CITY OF ROSES

Other books by Emily Isaacson:

Little Bird's Song

Voetelle

The Fleur-de-lis Vol I-III

The Sunken Garden (limited edition)

House of Rain

The Two Olive Trees

Hours From A Convent

Snowflake Princess

A Familiar Shore

CITY OF ROSES

EMILY ISAACSON

The Emily Isaacson Institute
Canada

Cover design and interior layout: Voetelle Art & Design
Cover photos © rockvillephoto and © Pavel.
License X by Fotolia.

Poems in *City of Roses* are derived from © Copyright 2013 *House of Rain* and *Snowflake Princess* by Emily Isaacson. The cloister series, Contemplations of Revelation is previously unpublished. May be reproduced for contemplative purposes.

ISBN: 978-1-312-82707-3

First Printing: 2015

Published by:

 The Emily Isaacson Institute
Canada

P.O. Box 3366
Mission, B.C. Canada V2V 4J5
www.emilyisaacsoninstitute.com

Printed by:
Lulu Enterprises Inc.
www.lulu.com
Printed in the United States of America.

To Peggy Claude-Pierre

Our bodies are our gardens, to the which our wills are gardeners: so that if we will plant nettles or sow lettuce, set hyssop and weed up thyme, supply it with one gender of herbs or distract it with many, either to have it sterile with idleness or manufactured with industry—why, the power and incorrigible authority of this, lies in our wills.

Shakespeare

Part I: Rose's Visit

Chapter 1

At half past seven every morning, Clare walked down St. Charles Avenue. The air was cold with the advent of autumn. The statue of St. Francis stood beside the fountain in the front garden. The large door swung open at her arrival, as geraniums on the stair staged a healing incentive. The hardwood hallway swung upward into a large staircase. There was a wooden bowl of satin rose petals on the landing. It was said that in Victoria, the gardens bloomed all year around.

Rose sat drinking red velvet tea on the chair in the living room. She had just arrived for a few months' visit. She stood to look out through the curtains. She watched through the window of one of the two Rockland mansions that served as the world-renowned eating disorder clinic, City of Roses. She knew the care workers were about to arrive.

A smooth even voice spoke behind closed doors. Rose felt the hum through the plastered walls, through the century-old paint, and wood moldings. The two mansions were as old as the early 1900's property they stood on, although well-kept. The hedges surrounded the property, guarding its secrecy.

Here there was a silence, like a vow. There was solitude, as a pensive thought. There were old ideas, old-fangled solutions, and the new ones that were merely alluded to. No one wanted to influence the patients when they were most suggestible. One could only explain that as one progressed towards wellness one became more objective and less subjective. That was all that was said.

Clare was Felicity's care worker. Felicity waited until Clare extended her hands, before looking up. The television was a monotone distraction, and one of the other girls did a crossword puzzle. When it was time to eat again, as it was every two hours, Clare would supervise the meal.

Pat placed some flowers in a vase. Flowers were atonement here on the grounds. They resounded of gratefulness in every room, filling the mansions with a scent of the flowering city. It was Pat who had once been Clare's care worker. Clare had been like an angel of mercy when she had first arrived as a patient at fourteen.

It was the desperate attempt of every mother to save her dying child that brought families, young women and even young men to the clinic. That desperation was born out of the months or even years of denial that everything was okay. When one finally turned around and saw a skeletal child in front of them, it was a cold awakening. There were many parents who had brought their daughters to City of Roses as a last resort.

The patients were here for six to nine months at a time for acute care. They were for the most part, young women with eating disorders such as anorexia and bulimia. It was a hands-on approach; one that required care workers around the clock. Care workers came on shift, and were always within arm's reach of their patients.

Could we gage the improvement over time? Rose knew that improvement came day by day, as color seeped back into the girls' cheeks. They ate like baby birds at first, and eventually learned to feed themselves. When they finally smiled, was the first day they were told, "You are well again."

City of Roses was the only in-patient eating disorder facility that provided such care, and had such a mandate. It told its clients of a future they would have, in the real world, with real people. Rose had felt the truth for many years now. She was a graduate of City of Roses. She knew City of Roses had an innate power to win the girls' hearts from stone cold and frightened, to warm and human.

How was this humanitarian place that rescued the paralyzed and terrified young girls from the psych ward and loved them back to life so eloquent? A woman held the lantern by night and made rounds of the children and teenagers sleeping under the down in their beds. Maggie, the founder, was the inspiration that the clinic under the eaves depended upon. The many suites of the mansions held young women who refused to eat, yet turned their heads and smiled when Maggie arrived.

A woman who appeared in the night, covered the miles of the ill, and disappeared with morning's light was the triumph of this fragile and eerie place. It was the eating disorder, the anorexia, that was like death. There was a coldness, a silence, just before someone who was starving themselves had given up completely. Only one person was unafraid to reach out, hug them, and take them in right at that moment when life and death hung in the balance.

There was a woman who knew this disease inside out, and could turn her patients around from death to life. It was Maggie, who had rescued her own two girls from the brink of starvation when they were teenagers. She proudly showed the picture of her daughter, Gabrielle, to each and every new patient. They all knew the story of how Maggie had learned to turn the condition around, by loving her daughter back to life.

Maggie knew and accepted each patient into the program personally. She embraced each one when they arrived on the doorstep. She oversaw each client's recovery. She knew when they were well again, and even let them return as care workers in the years that followed.

Rose had dark hair and features, yet light eyes. Maggie had known Rose for many years now. The light from the sun caught Rose's figure, leaving a shadow. Felicity looked up from the couch in the parlor. Felicity was sketching in her notebook. Her pencil scratched in the room, as she depicted the shadow world. She knew there was both fear and love in this place. There was the love that made you want to stay and the fear that desperately made you want to escape.

Felicity thought Rose made an intriguing muse; she bade her sit for a pencil portrait. Rose was handsome, somewhat as a medieval cottage, and Felicity could tell even at first meeting, that she never really went away, even though she had been gone a long time. If the gardens bloomed all year round in Victoria, Felicity drew that too. Her sketch pad was rich with the silvery penciled ideas of a Victorian spring. Victoria was rich in the reminiscence of the Old World.

Rose was from Europe, and had traveled through many cultures. The Old World was both relic and inspiration to her, and the study of languages in her home had been paramount. She had learned to speak English, French, and High German. Later, she was grateful for their soothing melodious words and tones. The cultures she had come in contact with had left her wide-eyed and intrigued.

The soothing voices never left her, now that she was an adult, now that she had many friends, relatives, and even a child. Rose was an assistant curator at the art gallery of Fussen, Germany. She was familiar with the art world, with its eclectic form and taste. Art had its sophistication and its eccentricities.

Rose spoke in warm tones to the visitors who arrived and followed behind the docent. She felt inspired at the monthly changeover of local artists and exhibits, and the local history of Bavaria. The New Swan Stone Castle was formally called "Neuschwanstein" in German, and towered on the side of the mountain.

An enchanting historical landmark, it was complete with spiraling towers and brilliant artistic depictions. The castle itself looked like it was something out of a fairy tale. The architecture featured beauty and elegance intertwined, and had created the inspiration for Walt Disney's fairy tale castle at Disneyland. Ludwig II originally ordered construction on the great building in 1869, but it was never completely finished.

The King had been a fan of Richard Wagner and the castle was named after the Swan Knight in Wagner's opera. Ludwig's love of the composer was quite evident as you walked through the castle's luxurious passageways; the many paintings hung on the walls depicted scenes from Wagner's operas. Rose's husband Friedrich Tuller was a German historian, and had showed her the castle many times, explaining its weighty history.

They had many times as a family, with their son Oliver, followed a road that ran across the countryside and featured beautiful old walled towns, deep fragrant meadows, and picturesque villages—coming to its end in Fussen, called *The Romantic Road*. What an end it was; looking out upon the hills and mountains of Germany was a moment in time that took Rose's breath away.

Rose usually sat in the large living room of the first mansion, listening to the other patients, conversing with the manager. Jack was Carla's husband and was an ambitious force of positivity behind the employees. He had invited her personally to return after many years to visit City of Roses. She was there for a few months to be part of the filming of a movie. Gabrielle had written a book about the clinic, and included her story. *Red Velvet Cake* had been many months in the making. A German producer who had been a friend of her husband was in town to begin filming the movie.

The memories came back quickly of being twenty-one and anorexic. She never thought she would fall prey to an eating disorder, but she had been only seventy-five pounds when she became an out-patient. Her parents were living in Victoria at the time. She had been dark-haired, with circles under her eyes, and an emaciated form from months of starving herself and over-exercise. Only water and coffee have no calories, she had noted. The thought of eating any food had frightened her. She cut up small pieces of cantaloupe for her daily meal.

That was seven years ago now. She no longer thought like an anorexic, but she did not forget that world of hunger and fear—the proud accomplishment of being thinner than everyone else, and the depths of depression that she would never be normal again. The mindset took a long time to leave.

The slippered feet of patients were silent over the creaking floorboards. Fruit was like a still-life on the table, and the rooms were filled with overstuffed couches and antique furniture. There were bright pillows and a fragrant scent of bouquets in the air. On the table was a vase of roses, amid the quiet conversation.

There was an art easel in the front room and a garden in the back. The care workers were sitting cross-legged on the stoop. Carla's dark hair was pulled back into a ponytail, and she chatted. They had just come off shift and would stay for awhile to have coffee with cinnamon buns.

"How to catch a wild horse?" Maggie, the director, queried. At the staff meeting Clare sat in the living room with the other care workers to discuss the details of a new arrival. Her name was Katy Ann Bird and she was coming from England to play a part in the movie. She was twenty-eight and was also anorexic. Katy Ann Bird looked young for her age. Katy would play the main character Ebony Velvet from the time she was a patient at City of Roses, until her death. Because Ebony was one of their girls who had not survived, it was particularly important to Maggie that her story be told.

The atmosphere was congenial and the twenty-five other care workers from all walks of life were casually dressed in jeans. They were the hands and feet of City of Roses, the clinic so successful for its one-on-one care model. City of Roses staff had been specially hired and picked for their gift of compassion. There was a spirit of camaraderie as they practiced coaching the patients through emotional ups and downs, through difficult meals, in role play.

"When the girls come as new patients," Maggie said, "they all receive specially selected bowls and cups of their own." Maggie had found the secret of the importance of treating each patient as an individual. She had also discovered her care workers were invaluable to her, the hands-on work that allowed her to help so many young women and men. There was a secret language evidenced in the emaciated bodies, in the hunger, and the denial of pain. Maggie had discovered it, and it had kept her up by night contemplating it. She knew what to say to assuage the condition until the sufferer was well. This she taught to them over and over again.

Chapter 2

Clare sat in the director's office the next day. She was to show Katy around when she arrived. She saw the Catholic influences on City of Roses as a blessing in disguise. They had pioneered a restitutional community that others could model. Maggie had invited Clare to stay awhile, under a tree that would not be cut down. The prayers over the mansion numbered in the thousands. A thousand people dreamed to enter its walls, the waiting list enumerated.

The black and white photographs, like birds under the stair, announced each client's progression toward healing. They were taken both when they arrived and when they were well. Maggie's archives contained hundreds of photographs of the clients who had once hidden in the shadows and now smiled. Their joy had returned.

When Clare walked into the room, any heart stopped. She had long braided hair that reached almost to her waist. She had recovered now, and the other girls followed her in the silence. She used to walk for six hours a day, like an African woman in the Sahara, searching for water.

"What is it about the nightingale, that you so easily sculpt its nuances?" Rose thought in admiration, "Love flies."

She contemplated the nightingales that Clare was known for sculpting out of marble. "The open market sells your art, what comes out stony and smooth, that you had discovered it among the roadsides of the Old World," Rose thought.

The nightingales were cold and dark to the touch. They seemed to sing out of the night. They sat high on vendors shelves at Market Square. Shoppers wandered by, eating fudge in white and dark chocolate. There were stickers of cherubs that the children would pull from rolls to buy. There were the more auspicious heads of passing art collectors; the nightingales caught their eye, like a song.

The full-time care and unconditional love for all human beings, but particularly their patients, was the model at City of Roses. All the care workers were trained to follow the method of reversing negativity. Clare also knew how important it was for the girls to eat every two hours to regulate their metabolisms. She would either make the food for them, or supervise as they made it. No detail of healing was overlooked.

"The time will come when suffering will not be viewed as an item to confine and medicate," said Maggie, the director.

Maggie's daughter, Gabrielle spoke, "Their emaciated faces do not mask pain. Their suffering is transmuted in the gaunt haunted looks, and the camera remembers it."

Pat responded, "When I come here and find a place to communicate with someone reminiscent of death, my character is emboldened by grace not to perform. I cannot but extend the genuine authenticity of a real tryst with kindness."

"We have a way with words that soothes over bumps and bruises. Somehow the wounding in life got them into this fragile place that they don't know how to leave. It is still and eerie, when they are as fragile as baby birds," said Carla.

"But don't forget the genuine smiles when they recover. That is what I wait for," said Maggie. "We receive the weak, and wait until they are strong."

Clare brings her yogurt and sits on the porch, always within arm's reach of her patient. The day is cool and the wind ruffles her hair, as she sits next to Rose. The clinic film, with a German producer, should appeal to Europe. The theme of healing anorexia from the ground up depicted in *Red Velvet Cake* was once of unconditional love in a negative culture. The producer is open-minded, and very interested in the inner landscape of a patient, their self-concept.

A week later, the girls sit on the red porch and the air is open and casual. The camera rolls and Rose watches the filming, from the book written by Gabrielle. From a well perspective, this looks good. The false premise that life is a hurtful place will change.

Polly, the clinic photographer, caught Felicity on film, under the grape arbor. Felicity has large eyes that transform pain into solace in the room. The life story of many of the anorexic girls reminisced of those bright red apples on a branch in the backyard. They were now willing to share it, while there was still time.

The clear juice of an apple ran down a little boy's face. His name was Jacob and he was four. The youngest member of the house, it was hard to believe that the eating disorder mindset had control over his thoughts. Yet he was convinced we would become overweight if he ate. His food intake had dwindled. Now, at the clinic in Victoria, he was beginning to recover.

"My mouth tasted the woody apples of your tree— their clear juice relinquished; the young sun on the river dapples the water with a glassy finish. Will the aroma be forgotten? Their bronzed grace, now reaching and holding with the lightest touch, staid, begotten," he recalled later.

When care workers sit on the green and watch the progress of those who are just starting out on the journey toward the goal, their courage grows. Soccer balls are kicked around the yard, and art lessons will follow. Somehow in the paint and paintings, in a peaceful corner of the house, catharsis will find its way to the surface. They know their charges will succeed, and no longer need to be successful.

Maggie stood looking over the pieces of acrylic art hanging on the walls of the art room. Each one had a message, and spoke of its author. There was pain, but there was also resolution. As the girls grew stronger their outlook changed. They were more alert, more hopeful, and could forgive. Their art became more positive, and they could bond with others.

Clare took the arm of her youngest patient and they walked around the yard in the afternoon break. Each child, teenager, or adult had a specialized program, which included some exercise. Acute patients were housed in suites in one of the two Tudor mansions that composed City of Roses, until they moved onto partial care in one of the other houses nearby. The patients typically graduated from the program when they were well enough to leave and go home. Some stayed and became care workers, like Clare.

The care workers would reassure the patients repeatedly when they ate. It was the only way they could build trust and keep the food down. As they gained the weight back, little by little, their skeletons disappeared.

Their smiles returned. They could remember what they wanted to do in life, and why. There was a reason for everyone to eat, and a reason for every child to live.

Clare was showing Katy around the grounds. Rose watched from a distance. Katy Ann Bird had dark hair and white skin, and was as slender as a twelve year old. Rose knew Katy would play Ebony Velvet. Rose didn't mind someone famous whom she had just met playing in the movie; in fact, it was a great turn of events. Katy was unlike Ebony; she was a gilded lily. She would be perfect for the part.

It was a thought in the back of Rose's mind while she stayed at City of Roses: the question was whether letting go of the disorder and starting again with a new construct was acceptable. What if one were to find that it did not mesh with modern society to be cured, or pass unnoticed by the local psychiatrist? That was something that was only all right on film. Otherwise it would be reprehensible. All their stories of recovery seemed to stop at this one point, and Ebony's continued on.

Rose thought, "Now the care workers sit in the living room and consider the anorexic and bulimic, the repercussion of the long years of starvation; but Katy Ann Bird will bring it to life."

Rose sat at the window of the mansion, contemplating. She was reading *The Philosophy of Hunger*.

She read, "*My philosophy of hunger as a needed traditionalist was one that ensured mealtimes, the pacifying of emotions, and wellbeing. Hunger to the anorexic was a staid*

fallback, a terrifying enemy, and reassuring familiar
companion."

Rose wrote in her journal:

*I stood with my back to the forest watching the sun's last fading
purple light, the once burgeoning moon, rising poorest from a
refugee camp in desert night, where the fire is the only
comfort—red as a mind contorted by the black fear of having
naught. The distance is now said to be a symbol of indifference
near death; but refusing to dream the future.*

The director smiled as Katy finished the tour of City
of Roses. She invited her into the office where she
counseled. The beautiful room with latticed panes and
overstuffed chairs mirrored the images of the many
patients who had entered here on their journey to healing.

Katy asked, "How does this all begin. What makes the
girls want to recover with their very souls?"

"There is much to look forward to on the other side.
When they let go of the former life, the one that
preempted the disorder, and start again with a new
construct—it is one that will last a lifetime. It is here. It is
now."

The invitation to Katy had been held out, and she had
accepted. The offer to do the film was not contingent on
her recovery from an eating disorder, but she had
concurrently been accepted into the program. In a year
from now, she too could be a graduate of City of Roses.

**Chapter 3**

Katy had a cold power when she entered a room. Their backs were always toward her, and the green and purple rustle of skirts was a distraction from the counterpoint of conversation. The fine china of teacups on saucers clinked with small teaspoons. Her head turned toward the window and the sun. She could see the vast blue sky through the bay window, the rose garden, and the organic plot of vegetables. A man coughed politely. The voices hushed to whispers.

The desserts were neatly arranged on plates, macaroons, small cakes, biscuits, and tea. "Just think, soon you'll be in the movies in Europe," someone commented. "Thank you," she replied.

"We're so fortunate to have you be in this film of the clinic. I always knew the City of Roses girls were going to be world famous. I don't see how we could have done this production without you. Here, have a cup of tea and a biscuit," Carla urged.

"Welcome everyone!" boomed a voice. "We are here today to celebrate the debut of the book *Red Velvet Cake,* by Gabrielle, and the beginning of filming by our German producer, August Leiland, his cherished friend, Rose, and star Katy Ann Bird. I would like to propose a toast to a successful book and an even more successful film."

"Thank you," August said. The others nodded and smiled.

"Katy, and Rose," said August. "Come up here. Say a few words."

Katy said cautiously, "On stage, when the audience is silent, and the curtain opens, there is a story that needs unfolding through the eye of one who has stood through the victimization of playwrights and rehearsals, of the conceptual theatre and the eye makeup smudges: the lines and lines, and the foreseeable moments of an impossible ship's mast. It rises before us, looming into the darkness."

"I believe we have now set sail," said Rose.

Gabrielle's daughter Helena was nine years old and hid behind her mother. Her dark hair was plaited and she wore her uniform from Catholic school. Gabrielle had been a model in her earlier days and her stance was somewhat imposing with long brown hair and hazel eyes. Her husband, Alistair, had been unable to come to the launch of the new film from the book he had sacrificed so much for. Gabrielle sat at the teak table to sign copies.

A violinist played classical music in the background. Gabrielle signed books and made soothing gestures. Everyone bought one, and most stood in line to have it autographed. She was there for over an hour, and then the crowd disappeared. She stood up to go.

"Thank you so much," said Carla, who had organized the event.

"You're very welcome," said Gabrielle, taking Helena by the hand. "I enjoyed it. I owe it all to our girls, they are very talented. It's time they had a voice."

When Gabrielle reached home, Alistair stood in the kitchen, pouring champagne into wine glasses. Gabrielle put the flowers she had received in water.

"How did it go?" Alistair asked.

"Beautiful . . . Helena and I had a wonderful time. I so enjoy being the author of a book people will never forget about the clinic and our girls," she said.

"It makes all the work well worth it," he commented.

"Let's go for a walk while it's still light," she suggested.

The three of them put on wool coats and went down to the park, where Helena fed the ducks. Alistair and Gabrielle sat on the bench and watched. The late afternoon become dusk and the light faded. They walked home along the street.

It was that time of night—and night was a winter of the soul, in which the stars crystallized like snowflakes— the streetlights began to go on, they burned a little bleary-eyed at first. The last of the children's toys had been amassed from the lawns, and the bicycles had been brought in from the sidewalks. There was a dark-haired woman in a white dress they could see through the window who was lighting a lamp against the night. As she gazed at them, and as she peered into the street, a last skylark flew past on its way to the fields, to the birds roosting high under barn eves on the outskirts of the city.

"I'm glad we found Katy Ann Bird to play Ebony Velvet," said Gabrielle. "She looks brilliant in the part."

"I too could not be happier with how things have gone, from the first imagination of a movie, to the reality of production," said Alistair.

It was her thought, passing by him, as a flitting nightingale of the Old World, a Luscinia megarhynchos, passing the dark-haired woman who nursed the miles of eventide.

The mystery of bird aerodynamics allured Alistair silently, reminding him of the automatic pilot Ebony Velvet's great-grandfather had built once, marking him as a famous inventor. Although he had lost his fortune in the stock market crash, he had managed to keep his beloved collection of oil paintings, including an original Monet. Gabrielle had mulled over this history amid casting Ebony Velvet as her main character. The suspense had built over time as she wove Ebony's story of both chosen and forced seclusion.

At home, observing a vintage lampshade in hand, Gabrielle was questioning the blue shadows and the light... *"that serenade the infant born in bright starched fabric cribs, the blurry tempest lands—the servant stands, beating the*

cooling palm," she quoted Ebony's last sonnet. She held the sculpture of the lamp's enameled base, *"athlete of all pertaining to the race toward morning—the resistance's oil balm, mother of this era. A busy throng moving on, smoky denouement in form, telling of the path beneath her feet, worn to candles from the lamp of moonlit song. Grassroots binding of the look from wasteful, to the cry for ancient things more tasteful,"* she recalled.

The next morning was like spring. Helena stirred almond milk into her cereal as her mother sipped herbal tea with stevia. Very slowly, the sun was ripening the air, as the pale indigo of a bluebell, to a fragrant fruit hanging from a celestial tree. The original screenplay for *Red Velvet Cake* was piled on the hardwood floor, marked over with a red pencil, amid library books. The piano was a honey-colored Samick, modern enough and in tune. Helena began her practicing before school, and continued for half an hour in preparation for her lessons once a week. Helena was Maggie's granddaughter, and regarded the work they did at City of Roses as golden and full of promise.

Noon was like summer. The sun was high and warm. Helena looked forward to the day when she would be able to work at the mansion also, even if it meant filing and answering phones. She had seen many commercials for organizations that helped starving and malnourished children in foreign countries, but now she realized that sometimes the hungry emaciated children were right outside the front door. She didn't have far to look to be of good to them just by eating normally. She knew she would eventually see them smile again at City of Roses on graduation day when their parents came to take them home.

Autumn was like evening. The sunset was the color of falling leaves. There was a time and place where people recovered, and although some stayed to work at the clinic, most went back to their lives, married and lived happily. It wasn't that the condition no longer existed, but they had learned to live beyond its clutches.

Rose stood in the garden of the mansion as the stars came out. There was a cool breeze ruffling the flowers. She moved like a shadow among the roses. "I never promised you, I never promised." she thought. Yet she had promised something.

"*The finely dressed garden shall display only the variant colors, fine, the clear trumpet of the eve shall play in pure even tone, sure as the sign that heaven broaches near the roses—and all of eventide listens in to find the sweet, in prayerful poses.*" Ebony had written those words.

Each flower variety held a particular significance to her. That is because Ebony had put a line of verse with each one, and it had been laminated to the post telling of its kind. "*The gardens of the night, now shadowed, still.*" she read.

 Chapter 4

The leaves swept her face like feathers. That evening, back at the girls' Pennywhistle House, Rose walked uphill. A storm was not yet brewing at the top. The day had crouched around Rose like a tiger; the myriad of moments, worth remembering or not remembering spanned a decade.

When she returned home, there was the obvious generosity of an orange, rolling down the hallway from Polly's room. As if no one were around, she picked it up with great curiosity. She savored its gift, as the sun was ripe fruit hanging from its bough. The moon was a woman doing her ironing. She pressed and starched it and hung it in the closet. When there were no more wrinkles, and no more shirts to iron, she shone her benevolence.

Rose was a nightingale at heart. In her field, there was a tree where the Old World thrush would sing. When she was a child, they had called her Kyrie Eleison after the mass. When she was older they had shortened it to Rose, as it sounded like an English name.

When she was nine and had arrived in Canada from Europe, she still could not speak English. She had learned quickly, copying the other children's syllables at school, watching their gestures. She knew her life depended on it. She wrote in blue ink on the white page, line after line. She followed the progression of teachable thought. She repeated the spelling of words and did sums, working out the round numbers with a Laurentian pencil sharpened to perfection.

Rose's mind was like a bird even then, and would flit past the schoolroom window. Even in shadows, the onslaught of rainy days and piles of high school homework, there were the birds. They would appear out of nowhere—a will that had not lost its ability to fly. Her thoughts were wing-tipped.

Rose read from Maggie's book, "*What drew me into the philosophy of hunger, resting my emotions from need and the burdens of want, was the returning again and again to my source.*"

When turns the weather to a fierce grey storm, Rose quoted in her journal, *we plunge into the cover of the trees, we reign in all our damp with leaf-light's keys, we take a liking to our dry thrift form. And for clothing, branches spar decorum, while flowers decorate the hair. The bees dance smitten o'er the green treacherously, now creatures of the woodland and the morn. We once wore dress within the looking glass and talked in shadows of the evening's lace; the sun-filled hours were traipsing to the dance in diametric meter of the class, we spun to charity of solemn face, and bowed to light, enamored in this spance.*

The old clock ticking in the Pennywhistle living room went on. The trains below the old house kept rumbling into the station. The tropical plants, lithe and green, wore reminiscence in the room. The girls chatted over tea and bran muffins in the mornings.

The island road stretched out smooth and flat before Polly as she bicycled toward the ocean. Her favorite spot was along Arbutus Road. There the arbutus trees leaned over the water, with red peeling bark and olive interiors. The scent of salt was euphoric.

Polly had lived on Vancouver Island since she was three years old with her parents, three sisters, and two brothers. There were so many children at home, that when she had gotten anorexia nervosa her parents decided she might stay at the mansion as an in-patient to be in the program. Six months later, at seventeen years old, she had moved into partial care; she now lived in Pennywhistle House downtown. Eleanor was their house mother, and came each morning at eight and stayed until they went to bed.

The house used to belong to the teacher from the conservatory. Music had permeated even the wallpaper, and there was still a piano in the living room. Eleanor could play Chopin, and had brought her Mazurkas and several Nocturnes. The girls would sit and listen in the evenings, wrapped in their afghans. They neglected to watch the television or even read the daily newspaper. The group of girls from the mansion in-patient program admitted they were sensitive to any negativity whatsoever.

Rose walked frequently with Polly in the old neighborhood. The trees were black charcoal etchings without blossoms. Polly lit a cigarette. The stoops, broad and peeling, invited a visit.

Carla had given her a rose to thank her for attending the opening. It bloomed for a week without fading. Rose's view of the movie was constant; she had been one of the first alumni of City of Roses. Rose had valued the opportunity to tell her story, as Gabrielle composed the original movie. The stories of many that had passed through their doors, were like ships that had finally set sail from a harbor. The producer thought he could win her favor by inviting her over from Germany to Victoria.

Polly made linguini on the old stove, but Rose could hardly eat. She swirled the pasta on her plate. The kitchen was blue with big windows. There was an occasional robin in the garden. Eleanor, the house mother, had put out bird seed.

Polly was the official photographer for City of Roses; she was in the midst of framing photos of all the patients. She took their pictures both when they arrived, and when they were well, nine months later. The portraits took place somewhere in the large backyard or under the grape arbor. The grape vines hung down over Felicity's blonde features. The photos were in black and white, or even sepia.

Rose mused. Her mind turned to one of Ebony Velvet's sonnets: *"Turn brevity to song and valor emanates from this—that the mind is theologically inclined to do war and battles forthwith. Take out one's sword, and triumph!—slay the foe at this last hour, when earth is falling low; into a field, death's horse now circles round and ends the rider's life on gravestone mound."*

The walls were sun-yellow. Rose had almost forgotten. When she remembered, it was a memory of being young and unwilling. Perhaps it was the staff at City of Roses that had made such a difference; who could make life changing decisions for someone like herself when she was young, so she would not forget what was really important to her about life. When she found what was really important, it was art—its portrayals and nuances. When she had chosen art as a career, she had for the first time felt that she was making the right choice.

Rose sat in the living room where the light was best. The stereo played languid jazz music. There were a number of books on psychology in the bookcase. Incense burned in the hallway. The tiny thread of smoke filled the room with sandalwood. The girls never tired of the smoky book nook.

Eleanor went over the hardwood floors with a mop and pine oil. She dusted the tops of the furniture. The second room was shared by Felicity and Hilary, and staying in the attic was Rose. The girls watched Eleanor water the

plants as they talked in the living room. They took their
vitamins which were kept on the counter. There was
fresh water from a spring Polly had found. She filled the
stone jug every week, and then made brown rice with the
water.

There was an antique store right below the house. It
boasted a brass bed, glassware, wooden trunks, and even a
dusty velvet cape. Hilary was looking for an early 1900's
writing desk and practiced writing for the newspaper on
an old typewriter.

"She is such a difficult child," Polly's mother had said
of Polly, talking on the telephone.

"Even if I made it," her mother said, "she would refuse
peach cobbler. All she drinks is very cold water."

That was nine months ago. Now Polly was about to
graduate from the program. Her mind was no longer
controlled by perfectionism. Better yet, the negative mind
had been silenced. She had been inspired by Gabrielle's
book *Red Velvet Cake*, and was delighted that they were
spending several months in a film shoot with Rose and
Katy.

"*Dance onward to the rhythm of my drum*," recalled Rose,
a quote from Ebony. "*Stand burnished in the bronze sunlight
of day; let the shadows sweep your soul by the way of the iris
and star it has come from. Jump at the chance to move to
purplish lore. As a magician would saw you in half, as the mane*

of a horse flies by the staff, come back from the brink of what made you poor."

The air smelled of salt as Polly neared the water. At the end of the road were the woods and the beach. She sat on the driftwood for a few minutes, arranging the shells and stones at her feet. Sunlight sanded the shore of her mind like a piece of driftwood.

The sea became smooth as liquid silver, companion to the earth and sky, salty and cold—the end destiny of every river. She had brought a banana; she would no longer refuse to eat. Polly liked to be alone so she could think. Solitude was her strength of mind. She would walk down to the island point.

Contemplations of Revelation

O true Child,
O true liturgy of birth,
O true song and troubadour,
O onward and inward growth,
Contemplate!

O only burgeoning invisible,
Unfolding of a flower's petal,
(respect, values, practices)
Destine!

O paradox of all forces of earth and heaven,
O irony of the sacred verse in rhyme,
Play!

O Rooted tree, deep within the ground,
O Ancient idea that breathes new life,
O Shores of endless seas within their bounds,
O Infant of the mother's breast,
O Milk of rich nourishment,
Dream!

Part II: Red Velvet Cake

Chapter 5

The theory of the wild horse was one that Maggie elaborated on at staff meetings from time to time. She had learned to be a horse whisperer around Sequoia, who had a horse of her own. Sequoia had come through the out-patient program before the in-patient facility was completed. No matter what, it seemed Maggie knew Sequoia best of anyone, and it had taken her some time to draw out the shy girl. Eventually Sequoia had come to work at the mansion.

Her clients knew that hunger was like a horse that needed to be gently and carefully trained by a worthy person they could trust. There was no one the girls trusted more than Maggie. Maggie's very wide dark eyes and porcelain skin always glowed with health, and she had an inner beauty that drew you to her face. It was always an honor to be called for a session with Maggie. The girls waited on the overstuffed couch outside the door for their turn.

Maggie was real and not afraid of pain. She knew if her anorexic girls started to eat again, they would begin to feel their emotions that had all but been numbed by starvation. Many of them lapsed at times into trances.

They were afraid to feel. They never wanted to be angry or upset.

"These children grow up with the world on their shoulders," Maggie remarked to Sequoia one day. "They cannot remedy it though."

"Do you remember the time I told you about Atlas, and how he carried the world on his shoulders," Maggie asked.

"Yes," said Sequoia. She remembered it well.

Her mind returned to the small office downtown where Maggie had started to counsel and put the gold letters on the glass window: *Eating Disorders Anorexia, Bulimia.*

Sequoia had spent many hours there, just quietly talking with her counselor and savior. It was always a given that Maggie had saved her life. Anyone who had been through the throes of an eating disorder could relate to the fear of the unknown, and future that seemed devoid of hope. Then there was that first meeting with Maggie, the moment of acceptance into the program, where she knew there was a way out, and took hold of the hope that she would recover.

Felicity had long blond hair, ruffling in the wind as she walked along the rose garden path. She stopped and noted each variety. She observed the pewter bird bath filled with water. She admired the petals, the velvet blooms of each individual one. What a delicate perfume there is here, she thought.

While Felicity and her twin sister Hilary were very much alike, only her sister was bulimic and she was anorexic. Her family had moved to Victoria so both girls could enter the in-patient program. She and her sister were now living in partial-care and came in to the mansion for counseling three days a week.

While her sister was in with the counselor, Felicity walked in the garden. She could read verses under each variety of rose. Ebony was a talented writer, she thought. Felicity was not religious, but she did not mind people who were. Each verse seemed almost a prayer.

"A Whiter Shade of Pale-Pink Hybrid Tea. *The light to bear at my humble last breath, the goblet of oil, cast out purest gold: all speak of favor's now placed laurel wreath—the best reward when I am creased and old,*" Felicity read.

Hilary was speaking behind the closed door. "When the wild horse becomes a cultivated subject, I will put my inner critic outside of my constellation. The voice that wants to destroy all I have lived for, will be a black hole in my galaxy: a voice of nothing, where no man travels. The voice even criticizes my mother. My mother was the first being that fed me, a wild horse at birth. "

Felicity walked along to "Albertine—Large Pink Climbing. *I shall with folded hands, resting, here pray for my* heart's desire to not be lost when I am gone, the print words to stop saying all that was delicate and austere then," Felicity read.

"I sat at the kitchen table, a muse, unblinking. I wanted more than three Ritz crackers, but I held them in my palm, like gold coins. They were my prize for being unyielding, unmoving, and defiant," said Hilary.

Felicity read, "Avon—Small White Ground Cover. *For I am but a savage beast, beauty in my time that cloaked a sorry pink smile (that chap stick almost choked with song's glory), in hunter's boots, and brought the deer from miles.*"

"When I the child ate, I was cherished, loved, and cared for. I grew strong, intelligent, and reliant. Surely there was a good reason to eat, to digest nutrients, to achieve health, to be strong," said Hilary.

Felicity continued on down the row.
"Breath of Life—Small Orange Climbing," read Felicity. *Blue as the bloom of petals, bright being translucent with the arm of paradise at my back, a mighty army, armor shod, a silver multitude without vice.*"

"I am now twenty, and have spent a few unwitting years in college listening to the other girls tell of diets. If I was staring in a trance, and from the point of view of a victim could no longer be awakened to my next meal, I know what brought me here. Once I could eat, and within a few years I was writhing at the thought. Curled up in a ball, my mother had stopped feeding me when I stopped eating. It was her fear of rejection, or her fear that I would be overweight if she forced it. She never did," said Hilary, "force me to see the issue or even talk about it."

Felicity continued along through the garden. "Burgundy Ice—Large other color Bush-cluster flowered/Floribunda. *Moving ever forward, no less vigor in their bones than the day they first set out to capture the castle of my heart strings,*" she read.

"If there was no hunger, there would be no desire, no seduction, no falling into temptation," said Hilary. "I may be reading between the lines," said her counselor, "but there is the terror of bulimia, and the ever-present enemy of anorexia, just as evidenced in your twin."

"You may know," said Hilary, "there is first the burn of hunger, the insatiable pain, then after awhile the hunger fades."

"Just as there is first the rejection of your starving child," said her counselor, "then the utter devotion, as a patriotism that we would die for. There is first the denial that we might lose, then the realization that we must fight."

"Canary Bird—Medium Yellow Shrub," read Felicity. *"And from the music of my soul will shout: I am no more about the little things."*

"A mother fights for her child as a moon in attendance of its planet. Her love and nurture will tame our wild horse. We will that the constellation of our souls continue in relative harmony, without disturbance," continued the counselor.

"Chandos Beauty—Large Pink Bush - large flowered/Hybrid Tea," read Felicity. *"Virulent as warm honey at midday, I taste the good of life here while it stays."*

"As long as there are two people who care, they will desire to feed each other. Feeding the family starts with this idea, and then grows it with each dependent offspring," said the counselor.

"Claret—Medium Red Bush - large flowered/Hybrid Tea. *The immortal being, watching death come as each proud red flower wilts, falls, and dies,"* Felicity read.

"The family multiplies nourishment to feed each child, and each child adores the mother for her dependable pattern, the rhythms of love and nurture, desire and contentment. Each child is sheltered by the father's strength and commitment, his protection and values," said the counselor.

"Dublin Bay—Medium Red Climbing," read Felicity. *"The light of each soul, therein proudly won to walk with you, hand in hand without lies that would obscure the spirit world..."*

"What is abuse, when there was no abuse in our home?" said Hilary. "Yet when people's inadequacies were mirrored in fear instead of trust, perhaps the vein of shame began with complacency."

"Felicite et Perpetue—Large White Climbing," Felicity stopped. *"Bequeath the fragrant eve's perfume with eyes that roam beneath the vast celestial skies and give the notion of sequestered will."* Felicity felt like a bird that drank only perfume in this garden.

It was Rose who had told her about the nightingale mind. There was an Old World thrush by the side of the road that sang at night. When she sang, Felicity knew she would remember the three mansions of the soul: heaven, earth, and hell. We were to stay in the two mansions of heaven and earth called City of Roses, thought Felicity.

The third mansion was too frightening to realize. Ebony knew about it because she had spent months in the psych ward, diagnosed with a mental illness. Felicity thought this must be the third mansion. It was a place where the doors locked behind you and you could not leave without a trial.

"Then there were moments of leniency, shadows of withdrawal. Highs of togetherness coupled with lows of aloneness and terrifying loneliness," said Hilary.

"Fellowship—Medium Orange Bush-cluster flowered/Floribunda," read Felicity. *"The covered head that bows before in prayer, speaks of enclosure: rays of truth, poverty's posterity and flowers, closed against the night's cool air."*

"Society runs like clockwork, never failing, never tiring, predictable as it is unpredictable, and constant as mother and father at providing resources," said the counselor.

"Freedom—Medium Yellow Bush—large flowered/Hybrid Tea" she read. *"The fountain of innumerable lights flickering in colors, indigo, rose. Wet mist, dripping off the end of my nose. The poise of every dancing spirit, bright. The moments of the sunken garden's verse allure the crowds so fond of sainted earth."*

"The wild horse of hunger is corralled by mealtimes, propriety, and carefully measured portions. The youth who have espoused the labor of the successful know they have left the rugged plains of the wild horses, for the calm, cool march of the subject," said the counselor.

"Princess of Wales—Medium White Bush-cluster flowered. *If only love would heal the fevered mind, but oil from roses soothes the heart in kind,*" read Felicity, reaching the end of the garden.

Hilary concluded, "I would one day rise from my sleep, unlike the earth between heaven and hell. The dark was shaking the victims of its hostility. There were savage predators looking for prey. I walked with a limp."

Chapter 6

When Felicity returned home, the three girls curled up on Rose's patchwork quilt on her bed in the attic. Their housemother was in the kitchen. They listened as Polly read from her journal of the last year. The entries of her adventures as a photographer made them feel that her perspective was her strength.

"*The lines were bright and steady as I readjusted my lenses, the tartan-sparse tree line a major chord to the rolling hillside. The art deco side of me always wants the shots to roll off with a painter's grain; something between future modernistic and impressionism—to hang on the wall in England would be avant garde. Ears still full of cotton, and a few coffees later I have a full roll of landscape, a stubbed toe and a few thoughts on why digital replaced the nuances of the fine lens au naturel.*

"*At the cultural festival, deep-fired elephant ears turn heads. The flowers of tradition bloom in elegant waltzes and highland dancers deepen their gestures for a rift in the crowd. When we have finished a roll for the Arts Society we turn on our hell-bent heels by the ocean. We sit at a cafe drinking Tazo all afternoon. Something is remote about this smashing beach.*

"*The shore generally coughs up all kinds of tourists, and the atmosphere is smoky like a sultry goddess. The condominium*

situation is rather expensive in this town, and a young doctor
could make a mint in family medicine.

"We hiked up the double edged mountain once with muffs
and mitts. The tips of our noses were blue-red with cold. The
rivers bent over in welcome because you drink and are unafraid.
When the director writes, everything is silent, and we are
unsure how many mass graves she contends with.

"The snow fields look lofty and distant but the visions are
candid. When there is injustice and we agree to remain silent
through some caucus consensus, the death grows. Death was
your enemy once, mother, and you fought it hand and foot on the
streets of Calcutta. Your enemy was your partner and constant
companion and you resisted the luxury. I choose to live: among
the dying who can only say, 'Yes, Mother Teresa.'

"We caught the peaks and life was heart-wrenching on the
way down. The twelve hour descent was a grueling portrait.
Once, we brought in the sheaves, and staring down the barrel of
a gun is a cold reminder. Whatever the trumpet section said, I
am stock still with fury.

"When my imagination failed, there was poetry. The seven
moons of Jupiter do not dwarf postmodernism in general. The
lines of verse do not replay a love or a splendor that grows
extinct with years. The general viewpoint is that long stretches
of field along country roads is as good a place as any to find an
old barn, an antique store, or an abandoned Emily Carr print.

"I clicked on an old shutter once, several times in a row.
Whatever came out was not worth my while unless you had an
empty wall. While you walk on the parapet, I pick up Dymer.

*The reefs of coral by moonlight are like hungry people to you,
scared and brittle—under the leaves of gold they wander."*

That night as she slept, Rose dreamed she was at City
of Roses. She had wandered outdoors for some fresh air
and followed the stone walk to the rose garden. Rose
found the garden empty of any other persons. The cool
breath of evening still lingered there. There was a shallow
pool surrounded by statues of stone women.

With a moment's wind on the surface of the water,
Rose looked in to the fountain and watched her reflection.
As she looked at the statues, she felt they were the stone
representations of her own inner heart. Everything was
calm and serene, no fluster or mayhem of the day marred
the garden of twilight where she could at last find her
sensibility reinstated. The last beads of sun had
permeated each floral leaf; the shadow-lights illumined
each flower with a ray of gold.

Rose felt that she would meet the sole gardener, but
there was no one in sight. That gardener was the guardian
of her emotions: each flower of anger, jealousy, love, or
pathos, whatever color it might be was hers. He tended
them, and they grew beneath his steady hands. Somehow
she felt that if they met, even in a dream, they would
know each other.

Rose could sense there was something lyrical yet
transcendent about the garden, drawing her like a magical

flame. Something about the garden and its statues was speaking in the night, and she felt its cold civility and ardent immortality both at once. The seasons, the days, and hours often spoke themselves through books she read or verse, and she was well-read as well as curator. Yet it had not before spoken to her in such fervency through her dreams.

In the fantastical depth of night, she awoke, still remembering the dream and its meaning. She promised herself to walk the stone path the very next day. Lighting a candle, carefully, she wrote down as much of the dream as she could remember. The ink scratched in her meticulous handwriting on the pages of her cloth-bound journal.

I believe the character of Ebony Velvet, she finished, *has much to say about modern society. Without understanding what created her skill as a poet and author, we might not understand the flight she took from the cold scientific viewpoint of the naturalist. She warmed the nature she observed with her poetic descriptions and astute observations. She always likened everyone to her subject, and thus wrote out human nature as a skilled artisan would.*

The writing itself, and the art Rose knew well, both equated themselves to the transformation that was required to become a spiritual being. Was it the poet who turned iron ores into gold? Rose could only surmise that this was an ancient way, known to every people group which espoused written language. It was a path forged toward the summit of a mountain that eventually others could follow, looking for transcendence. The view from the top won over even the harshest critic, afraid of his own shadow.

She recalled her Fairy Tale Prince, Ludwig, who had captured her imagination with his magnificent New Swan Stone Castle. His home had been the epitome of neo-romantic style. Not only that, the famous German castle overlooked the picturesque Hohenschwangau valley, only a short distance from the town of Fussen where she was curator. That had allowed her and Friedrich many impromptu visits. She was always awed at the ornate décor that had emanated from his visions.

She would not forget that those who are gifted see into the next world. Either with eyes of insight, or through literature, they would see beyond. They knew how to commune with poets through the ages of both past and future. They also incited the anger and treachery of those around them. Construction was halted on the castle and King Ludwig II was removed by power due to intrigue within his own cabinet.

The King himself was rarely concerned with matters of state and was sometimes thought to suffer from hallucinations. Her husband had told her that under Bavarian law, a King could be removed from power if he were found unfit to rule. The cabinet produced this report and the King drowned that day in the lake. However, Ludwig's mysterious death—ruled a suicide at the time— suggested that the cabinet was not content to merely remove him from power. Rose found this bit of mystery made the atmosphere of Neuschwanstein towering on the mountainside one of the most intriguing of the castles in Germany.

Many of the rooms in the enchanting castle had remained bare. Only fourteen rooms were finished before Ludwig's death. Yet the beauty of this famous German castle to Rose could not be denied. She believed in the authenticity of Ludwig`s vision, guiding his fondness for architecture and art, his love of poetry and opera.

"The sun reflects magnificently off its pearly walls," she thought. Inside the throne room was the picture of opulence with its intricate frescos of angels and other Christian depictions. She was determined to prove that his death was not a suicide. Her fostering of understanding in others was not in vain.

Transformation to understanding was the process she had in mind. She was only one person—if only one person can make a difference in the world. As she walked through life, she went from being the subjective victim of her emotions to the objective listener of others. She could now reach out with empathy when others needed her to understand them. This was what Rose experienced from the first day she came to City of Roses. It was the goal of therapy to help each patient understand this, so they could understand what made others think and act the way they did.

Rose knew this well when she sat at her desk in the art gallery and received each new exhibit. The flowers of artists' emotions were both modern—aesthetic, and postmodern—eclectic. The artists painted themselves on canvas, sculpted, drew, and wrote themselves into being. There was a formality about art. It was both a historical landmark, and authentic to its author. No other person could create exactly what you had created, in its originality.

She could say the same about City of Roses. Therapy was a formal design, a restructuring of the soul to hold its treasures. To be an architect of a human being required instilling it with both virtue and reason.

Rose had felt at the moment she graduated, that City of Roses had changed her forever, giving her the tools and resources to be a person. There was autonomy that was learned from age one, but then there was a host of things that blocked its progress, including other people. These blocks to autonomy and understanding had to be unlearned.

Ebony Velvet was the inner poet of City of Roses. As she wrote, the landscape changed for each of them. A plant, flower, or tree appeared. A brush with antiquity occurred, as history became the father of the past, and pathos became the mother of the future. The Fairy Tale Prince had commissioned her as the poet of his castle.

She would never be forgotten.

Chapter 7

Carla walked around with a clipboard. Jack made sure that the care workers carried pagers at all times. Rose had been told that Maggie was preparing to make a trip to England to promote the new film. She could see over the fence, looking out. She saw that in the garden next door, there were seven swans. They represent royalty, she thought to herself.

"*The swans that swam round the navy pond, all there resting in white apparel, pale in shadows, ivory as snow beyond the emerald mountain,*" she quoted.

The swans next door rose into the air.

"*The meadow vale,*" recalled Rose from the garden swing, "*bedecked with every lace flower, every hue—their feathers fluttered lightly in this light: the falling orange, magenta, sunset for one more evening. While the lead bright up and flew into the beauty of day over and becoming night. The darkness rested on the swans that swam in starkness, lavishing the ground beneath which I lay, with spray of petals from every nation wishing me farewell upon my station.*"

There is something we do here that is different from everywhere else," Maggie said to the care workers in succession, until they knew it off by heart. "We love people back to life."

No one else quite laid claim to this truth, and its practice quite like Maggie. She made sure she knew everyone inside out; her job depended on it. It was a philosophical strength to hold to your beliefs until they healed others, and others were healed in her presence. They eventually traded the false construct of anorexia for Maggie's philosophy of hunger. What was so convincing about City of Roses? Its theory and practice were delineated in the person of Maggie and all who emulated her.

Sequoia was tall and slender, with large eyes and small bones. She carried herself like a horsewoman, and controlled the large animals with a gentle hand. It was Maggie who had played a second parent to Sequoia, spending hours with her in session from the time she was a young teenager until she graduated from high school. It was Maggie who had presented her with a dozen white roses. She emulated Maggie in many ways, and had become a care worker at City of Roses at seventeen.

There are two commandments at City of Roses," Maggie said to a room full of care workers. "One is to accept yourself as you are; the second is to know that God accepts you as you are." It was Christmas at City of Roses. The tree in the center of the room touched the ceiling with silver and gold decorations, with riveting white lights.

Gabrielle read a letter from Ebony Velvet:

The white sun of winter spears the sky, as traces of frost ice the panes. The browned landscape covets snow as a sparkling covering, as the ponies are covered in the stable. The holly and silver are interspersed with red berries and flickering candles, burning the flavor of balsam into the wood house.

Green cedars in a mist of translucence, red said Christmas, white said purity of a child. Hay in a manger, I arrange the finishing touches on the nativity at the front of a long chapel. The choir will sing, and children traipse, dressed as angels with heavy wings and gold-strand hair, through the songs, away now from the dark in the tapered wicks of incarnation.

"Christmas is a memorable time for our clients. Being away from their parents and friends, when they are so fragile, means we make Christmas a special day," said Maggie.

Evelyn, Sequoia's mother, would come in and make the girls turkey. The girls would eat with their care workers in their separate suites. Then they would open presents together. All the parents of the in-patients had sent gifts ahead of time.

On Christmas day, the partial-care patients came over from Pennywhistle house. They were excited to participate in the day's festivities as planned. Polly, Felicity, and Hilary sang a piece they had worked on. Eleanor played the piano to accompany them.

A bowl of mandarin oranges sat on the coffee table. The other girls and boys opened stockings and gifts. Suddenly there were mounds of ribbon and wrapping paper. The warm temperatures of Victoria had begun to drop and traces of snowflakes were seen at the window.

"It may be a white Christmas after all," Alistair remarked.

Helena sighed wistfully as she carried a tray of coffee cake from the next room. Gabrielle followed her with steaming tea. The girls curled up on the overstuffed couch, a few ventured smiles. Even little Jacob looked content.

Sequoia was only eleven when she was the eldest of four children, on the yellowed stretch of property where a heritage house stood right on the outskirts of the city of Victoria. On one side you could see the mountains; on the other side was the country road that led to the homestead. Her father was J. William Hastings and ran a publishing house. He had a literary mind, and had raised his oldest daughter to have a love of literature.

Evelyn had waited for her daughter to return from the field when the sun went down. Her daughter's golden horse *Aurora* was her self-esteem, apart from the voices that criticized and berated her. The tyranny went on year after year as her daughter became a teenager. Yet, in spite of it, her gentleness and spiritual demeanor made her a favorite with people and animals everywhere she went. Sequoia had the potential to grow into a successful woman, even though her eating disorder had become more and more apparent to others, including her fellow students.

Evelyn, after five years of watching her eldest daughter refuse to eat, saw she had dwindled to a skeletal weight. She had finally taken her to a doctor, psychiatrist, dietician, and naturopath to find help. It was utter desperation that led her to City of Roses. She had heard City of Roses took on the worst and most severe cases; they were a stopping place for the desperate parents of eating disorder victims, and their phones rang with clients waiting in line from all over the world.

"Playing God," Maggie called it when they took on yet another patient who was as fragile as a baby bird and had to be spoon fed. Another person whose life hung in the balance was a risk to the program, but they took it on willingly, knowing that there was for these girls, no other recourse.

"How do we know who to save and who can wait?" Maggie thought.

Anorexia and bulimia, until the present, had seemed like an affliction of upper-class society. Now, right and left, it was crossing lines. More and more, young men and women of all ages were lacking nutrition education to refute its arguments. If they could formulate reasoning in their minds with which to eat, Maggie believed this would help them fight the condition.

Even beyond this, there was no point in harboring guilt over eating anymore once you came within the reaches of City of Roses. Accepting yourself and others was a way of life that allowed for the casual demeanor of the manager, director, and staff. A pair of jeans with a jacket was the common look, and most staff with charges carried pagers. They not only kept within arm's reach of their patients, they paged Maggie on a moment's notice if anything went wrong, a schedule changed, or the patient had a problem with their food plan. Patients attended their health appointments in town with their care workers.

Precautions had to be emphasized. At any moment a patient could try to run away or attempt to harm themselves. Patients had been known to hide to avoid eating. They would hide food in napkins, in their pockets, in their mouths, or even in the plants. The constant and ongoing education of loving people back to life, giving them the courage to eat again, had begun.

What seemed normative for most people, they realized could not be taken for granted. Especially around an eating disorder sufferer who had lived on a starvation diet for months, or even years of their life. The time they had lost could not necessarily be returned to them. It was the nutritionist's perspective at City of Roses that the effects of starvation could never be reversed. She had seen the consequences on the brain, on the thoughts, and on the emotions. Even though clients could gain the weight back, it was years before the fear of being hungry dissipated.

There was a dependence on the program, on the food plan, on the staff not only for positive feedback but for a new construct to replace the old. This would recreate a normal reality that included food in healthy portions and with appropriate nutrients. Maggie always said that if you take something away from someone you have to offer them an alternative. In response to anorexia, she would provide them with a model they could follow: it was how to live graciously. It was not to bite the hand that feeds you.

Maggie was the one who taught her clients how to understand others. She included an explanation of those who could not relate to the sensitivity of an eating disordered patient. She taught how to gage someone's empathy level. This helped them be objective.

The snow was falling. A woman entered the flower shop on Fort Street.

"A bouquet please," she said.

"Yes, madam."

"I'd like something purple, simple, and not too flowery."

"We have purple roses, irises, and hydrangeas."

"Roses would be fine."

"Perhaps some ivory baby's breath with that? Is it a special occasion?"

"No—just a thank-you."

"All settled then; would you like a few or a dozen?"

"I'll take a dozen of the very best, with baby's breath interspersed."

"Very good." The florist nodded.

She paid for the flowers.

He arranged the purple roses, wrapped them in tissue paper, and then put the bundle in her arms.

Her eyes shone, her shyness disappeared. Her skirt swept the floor as she turned to leave.

"Good-bye," he said. "Best Wishes."

The woman with the Armstreet cape covering her head of chestnut disappeared into the street. He had never seen her before; but one never knew on Vancouver Island as there were many tourists.

Jessica turned the corner and walked down St. Charles Avenue. She passed the pastel crepe-paper colored mansions on either side of the street, until she came to Rockland. The large mansion with the red staircase was set back from the road.

Maggie gestured to invite Jessica in for her appointment. She was a young lawyer who had succumbed to bulimia at thirty and was now a patient at City of Roses. She had grown up in Victoria and her parents lived at Pooley House, a large Tudor mansion that was once a hospital.

Maggie read over Jessica's food journal.

"Did you write anything else this week," Maggie asked.

Jessica held out a piece of paper to her, hesitantly. "I also wrote this," she replied.

You caught me picking red raspberries in the white snow once. A drop of my blood fell in the mansion of the earth. I had a warm heart and icy fingers. I grew cold, then fiery; a gold saffron wood became my iris. The silvery icicles hanging from the trees were my winter tiara.

You gave me an invitation.

I will live, with the canes and the stakes, with the seeds and the sweetness, biting my lip. Each boreal snowflake unique and priceless; each word around my throat, a stone of virtue. The architect of my life, one of surprising staircases and unbidden landscape art.

If I live in this mansion, it doesn't exist; the earth has put on a natural face and swallowed me like a raspberry in January. A robin red-breast would be expected twittering on the branch, come spring. But this, a fruit of the unexpected: I called for a song, and a symphony appeared, holding its breath. The Moldeau rushed as a river of notes, through barrenness and birth.

We walked on the wooded path to the sanctuary of our hearts, where the blood beats wild like a tangle of vines, and calm are the waves offshore. The lake of time had a far-away look in its eye, spying a fish in a bowl.

"Thank you, Jessica," Maggie said. "I will treasure this."

Chapter 8

As for her character—Ebony—when she was skeletal and pale, she was truly beautiful to Katy. But it was a slow painful death. Starvation was one of the most painful ways to die. Katy thought that her character's suffering was for the most part, overlooked. She looked at her script.

Playing an eating disorder victim was playing a modern muse. The stringencies of diet, and the argument of life versus death voiced themselves daily. "I want to inspire people," Katy thought, "so they understand why they need to be well and how. I finally have someone to point the way." Maggie understood eating disorders like no one she had ever met before.

Katy was like a flowering tree by the sea, even in her thin state. She had a conscience that reacted to controlling people, and she viewed all those who had tried to force her to get well as ignorant. They were dangerous, they used force and compliance. They did not ask her permission, they did not care what she thought.

It seemed like a miracle that she had found City of Roses. The care workers knew something about empathy that she had not experienced from her doctors or psychiatrist back home. Katy wanted everyone to know that there was now a better way. When she understood a concept, she knew it for life. Now she would be Ebony in person.

After the celebration of the book's debut, and the local filming on the grounds and at Hayward Lake, they would fly to Los Angeles to complete the scenes of Ebony in hospital. She understood the script in its entirety, as well as Gabrielle's approach to the story. If you could portray one person with accuracy, everyone would understand that singular story and its convictions.

"Cut."

"Ebony is a dying swan, Katy. She knows how to live in this movie, but she is essentially a martyr so we all come to grips with the truth. We have to understand that the world without Maggie's perspective of unconditional love would be a place we don't want to live," said the producer.

"Take one."

The cameras rolled. Katy was Ebony. She looked and felt the poet who had sent everyone scurrying on more than one occasion. Directors ran to the phone every time she had been hospitalized. Though she had been a patient once at City of Roses, Ebony walked into the real world and found herself misunderstood.

Even when it seemed she was abandoned by all but the system, they had watched from afar. They knew Ebony was a story that no one would forget. It was as if Ebony had known from the beginning that her place in the psych ward had significance, for she was not like the others. By that, Katy meant, Ebony had rehearsed as if for a role. In return, Katy played her muse with strength and understanding. She was a conceptual artist, and Ebony was her subject.

"Cut."

"Let's remember that most of what happens around Ebony is a depiction of her inner landscape. Her life as a naturalist, her journeys around the lake, and her relationships may be one-sided if we don't consider that they are as painful as they are fulfilling," said the producer.

"Ebony is sentenced to a psych ward then repeatedly diagnosed without her permission. As an involuntary patient, her situation is gripping and frightening. How could someone so knowledgeable and compassionate be hurt—particularly someone who knows Maggie and is a graduate of City of Roses.

"It tells us that someone is very much at odds with the work of City of Roses and what they do. If I didn't know better, I would think someone was trying to hurt Maggie in person."

"Ebony at this point looks like a pawn to the system. But she has much more influence and is weightier. She may in fact, be the white queen on the chessboard," said the scriptwriter.

"Take two. Rolling."

Katy is a patient at City of Roses. As Ebony, she will
have sessions with Maggie, and recover from an eating
disorder. They will film her actual sessions and recovery.

"Cut."

"To play a dying swan, one must be strong yet
beautiful. Elegance, in spite of inner turmoil and outer
suffering. Katy is the poet Ebony, although she has not
yet come into her full powers as a writer and been
published. She has not yet tamed her hunger, and it may,
in fact, be her mortal enemy," said the producer.

"Take three."

Maggie kindly reaches out to Katy, and draws her
toward her recovery with reassuring moments as she
learns to eat again. It is a slow process. Maggie will
prescribe distractions and positive reassurance until Katy
is well enough for counseling sessions.

"Cut."

Katy eats every two and a half hours just like all the
other patients. They stop for five minutes so the crew can
have a coffee while she has yogurt and sliced papaya with
her care worker. Her constant companion is kind and
reassuring. Katy knows that the new girls will eventually
be able to make their own food and eat without help.

"Take four."

"The movie *Red Velvet Cake* can't help but portray the
disease of the upper middle class. Those who seemed
immutable on many levels have for many years, both in
secret and on the front of magazines, watched their
daughters starve themselves to near-death. They are

controlled by a diet saturated culture that believes eating makes people fat. Young girls are afraid to eat properly. It is a culturally acceptable norm to go on a diet, and even try every diet on the market. Yo-yo dieting is common," says Gabrielle.

"The difference with the anorexic is they really believe they deserve to eat nothing. There is a lapse, where the condition will not be happy until they weight zero," says Maggie.

Maggie knows the mindset. She sees the cultural anorexia, the subclinical anorexia, and the emaciated forms in front of her that desperately cling to life while floundering in deep waters.

"Cut."

"Katy, you can trust Maggie. She knows what she's doing. She's walked her own difficult journey from death to life with her own two daughters. She's survived some of the most difficult situations a woman can face in her lifetime. It only makes her stronger. She is stronger inside than the condition that wants to hurt you."

"Take one."

Maggie says, "The condition affects many people, many children and adults. It may talk in your head. But they are lies, and I am telling you the truth. You can eat, and you will not get fat. You can have a high metabolism and will eventually be able to eat what you want, just like all the others who have passed through these doors."

Katy rocks back in forth, in clear distress that she has eaten something she thinks is fattening that day.

"What if I gain weight?" she says.

Maggie replies, "Honey, let me hold you. Someday this will all be over and you will be well."

"Cut."

Katy sees it. Suddenly she is faced with a woman who has the strength to reverse an entrenched eating disorder. Maggie is not intimidated by anorexia. She does not suffer from fear. She knows the way through. Katy knows Maggie is the woman lifting her lantern in the night as she makes her rounds. Katy, as she plays Ebony, will be watched over carefully, and loved back to life.

"Take two."

"I want to eat, but I can't," Katy says.

"I'm right here. I'll help you sweetheart," her care worker says. Sequoia makes the food for her charge's next meal and sits with Katy while she painstakingly eats. No one can be in the room. Katy insists on being completely alone with her worker. She doesn't want anyone to see her eat.

Every morning, Maggie will weigh her backwards on the scales. Katy will never know her weight. It is too much for the anorexic mind, which would hurt her if she did know a number. Katy cries at this. She wants to have a number in her head. The pain seems unbearable. Maggie knows, and strokes her cheek.

"Cut."

"As you get better, you will have plenty of outings. We will even let you go with Maggie to Pagliacci's and listen to the live music by her husband. He's a gifted violin player," says her care worker Sequoia.

"This is an outing that Maggie's girls love. They can order something on the menu. They have the opportunity to navigate with their newfound powers and eat in a public setting," says the producer.

"You will love Pag's," says Sequoia.

Contemplations of Revelation

O true Mother,
O true circle that surrounds,
O true love that bore,
O spirit of nourishment,
Rebirth!

O only door
into the realms of the earth and nature,
(mountain, river, and sea)
Release!

O Midwife of life and all its richness,
O Sewer of the stitched tapestry,
Order!

O Servant of the family way,
O Observer of the baby's play,
O Baker of the leavened loaf,
O Helper of the cooking fire,
O Wine of eventide is poured,
Walk last behind the child!

Section III: A Diverse River

Chapter 9

Maggie was in a double-bind. It was a locked white gate, but when she stretched out her hand, it suddenly opened. She was leaving the cathedral where she had asked the priest to light a blue candle. It was an act of intercession, a silent prayer for her most fragile client. The skeletal figure who had come over from Scotland needed a healing prayer said over her.

Maggie brought all her girls from death back to life. It was an act of sacrifice, for the time and effort required to mend the wrong done. It was a process of restoring joy. Even more, it was an acknowledgement of the person's deepest core.

Maggie's husband was of the firm belief that anorexia needed not just a personal response, but a community response. He had said on more than one occasion that a restorative community created a healing voice. He knew that the condition was not just a stricken child of white upper-class society anymore. It afflicted both men and women and was no respecter of persons.

"The community that caused the wound must heal the wound," he said of society. It was society's elite who responded. Suddenly Maggie was in demand at medical conferences around the country. She was invited to speak on panels, and on television. Even Oprah called Maggie an angel on earth.

It was a sunny afternoon when a prestigious looking envelope arrived with the red and white insignia of Buckingham Palace. Maggie had received an invite to visit Princess Diana. Diana requested her counsel as a private expert on anorexia and bulimia. Maggie responded promptly by booking a flight to England.

Maggie's trademark was being approachable. Everywhere she went, she wore jeans and carried a pager. Her girls at City of Roses knew how she presented her method of curing anyone who came within arm's reach. She knew more about unconditional love than most people learned in a lifetime. Was it not Maggie who had to fly in the night with her two young girls once—to escape the husband she had married young, only to be battered? Maggie had a strength that shone beyond her fragile eyes and porcelain skin.

When she returned, the girls surrounded her excitedly, chattering. They wanted to hear all the details of her brush with royalty. Wisely, Maggie kept the details to herself, and said little. Later she went over the event of her meeting with her husband.

It had been a quality time over tea at the Kensington. Diana had often offered her insight into humanitarian situations, and extended it as their visit was coming to an end. She encouraged Maggie to let the tree of their organization root deeper. She told of the roots of the restorative tree being the values of diversity and inter-connectedness. Maggie had been such a help to her, and she had given of her wisdom.

Maggie agreed, as did her husband on her return, that they must consider all the angles of humanitarianism. Within a few weeks, Maggie and Jack decided to hire a First Nations nutritionist. They could use the assistance with food plans, and the girls frequently had questions about health. Maggie could no longer do all the nutrition work alone.

The new nutritionist was named River. She had trained in restorative justice and circle keeping. Something of the Nootka band ran in her veins. It was the voice of the poet.

Maggie introduced River at the next staff meeting. They were interested in her unique holistic approach. Jack had had an idea. He felt that River should teach the staff how to conduct a traditional circle with a talking piece. They would sit in a clockwise circle, and go around the room, passing the talking piece one by one to the person speaking. That would give them all time to talk, and time to listen.

When River explained circle keeping to the staff, they understood at once. Maggie encouraged them all to share from the heart. Jack asked River what talking piece she would use. She took out an eagle feather, a symbol of strength, vision, and flight.

"Chief Dan George once said, 'My people's memory reaches into the beginning of all things,'" River began.

"Many times in life, we may have to return to the beginning to uproot the wrongs that have been done." River passed the talking piece clockwise to Clare.

"In a healing journey, we might be taking a walk on a familiar stretch of shore, perhaps one that you walked on many times as a child," said Clare.

Sequoia nodded her head in agreement as she received the talking piece. Her family knew well the many shores of Vancouver Island, the rocks that spoke, the sea that sanded with its salt spray. "The seashells are the poems, the house of wisdom of your people," she said. "People can either take them or leave them. They were written by dreams and calls in the night."

Others nodded their agreement. Those who grew up near the ocean knew its familiarity, its relentless pull of tide, and limitless depth. "We must in many ways return to the sea which is our home. The seashells were once houses of our soul," said Gabrielle.

"River is a woman whose voice is now heard in our restorative community," said Pat.

"We cannot remain a wounded nation any longer," said Maggie's husband.

All eyes moved to Alistair as he stood. "The First Nations People of Canada are a poet's voice that speaks like the sea. Many rivers run from the mountains to the salt of the ocean. They cannot be restrained, starved, or held captive any longer."

Eleanor continued, "They have taken the poet's voice out of the bentwood box. The poet's voice speaks."

They would have many more circle experiences with River. It was Maggie who initiated that the staff meetings be held in circle format from then on. Even though they used a different object as talking piece every time, the circle dialogue went on as before. It was a model to follow.

Maggie remarked to Sequoia one day as they watched through the window of the sunroom. A care worker held the elbow of the new girl from Scotland. She was still pale, but just beginning to smile. "Individuality and personality are both submerged when someone has an eating disorder."

"Yes," said Sequoia.

"How do we know if that person has been victimized?" asked Maggie. "Even in our desire for someone's life to have a happy ending, we can't refuse to accept the wrongs against them," she continued.

"It's possible that many of them have been victimized," said Sequoia.

"Not only that, they are highly sensitive people, with great empathy," said Maggie.

"That sounds like pathos—when you are sensitive enough to bear the burden of another," said Sequoia.

"In the modern world, we call it burden bearing," said Maggie. "But indeed, that is the nature of the sensitive child; they have a measure of pathos."

"It also seems they have an internal perpetrator who hurts them for eating," Sequoia said.

Maggie identified it. "That's the negative mind," she said. "It won't let them eat."

Maggie had vision and a strength that many recognized. It made her a force of change unlike Florence Nightingale. She alone was making reforms that would bring the psychiatric community into the present age. This would have a ripple effect, based on her altruism, everywhere she taught throughout the world.

Maggie knew that taking on high-profile clients like Ebony Velvet and Katy Ann Bird brought attention to the clinic. They were often in the local newspaper. It was somehow publicity they did not need or want. It was Ebony's poetry they wanted, and they followed her like a child would their mother.

"I am thankful that poetry—even skylarks and daffodils—is not sugar-coating," said Sequoia.

"It speaks of a void that asks for redemption," said Maggie. "It means we must learn from our mistakes."

"Does life have a happy ending?" Sequoia asked.

"When I asked Jessica to be our lawyer, and River to be our nutritionist, I believe it made restorative justice something that applied to mental health. Jessica would tell you that her values encompass compassion, diversity, and meaningful interactions. She has changed how I see interventions. River would say that the flower that blooms in her soul is not secondary, but from the seeds of the Divine in this world and restorative justice," said Maggie.

"Even from the broken pieces, there is a calm mosaic," Sequoia thought.

"Jessica's forgiveness of the world is represented by flowers," said Maggie. "You would not know that inside she was once bulimic. She was a wild horse who dug in the garbage bins for food, and then forced herself to throw up."

"I was anorexic but never bulimic, growing up," said Sequoia.

"You never hesitated to believe me when I told you you'd get well," said Maggie, "but many patients do."

"If they doubt you, they don't realize your intuition is guided by the stars of your constellation, as my mother would say," Sequoia remarked.

"Yes. It is the darkness, the wrong things that have happened to you, that makes the stars appear. I do know that," said Maggie.

Chapter 10

Maggie was speaking to Sequoia in confidence in her office. The leaded panes reflected the afternoon. A bouquet of flowers warmed in the sun. Sequoia sat in a chair opposite.

"I do know what it means to fly in the night. I left my husband once who would berate me and beat me in front of my two young girls," Maggie said. "I was raped several times and could not endure it. We escaped.

"First one daughter, then the other, got anorexia. When Gabrielle was anorexic she looked like this—" Maggie held out a picture of Gabrielle at sixteen. "I would just hold her. I did not know what else to do but love her back to life."

Sequoia listened carefully to Maggie's story.

"The psychiatrist would not take her as a patient. He said it was my fault. He thought that she would not live at seventy pounds. I slipped tiny morsels of food to her so her mind could gradually accept it. In a restaurant, I would feed her under the table. Little by little, she recovered," said Maggie.

"Now she works here with you at City of Roses," said Sequoia. Gabrielle had one daughter, and was now pregnant with her second child.

"The girls I invite with me to Pagliacci's are equally frightened at first. But my husband's band plays live music, and it is a warm caring atmosphere," said Maggie.

Mental health interventions abounded in the field, but those who performed them were already looking for an integrative response. Particularly with eating disorders, professionals were looking past just re-feeding a starvation victim to real transformation. Those who heard Maggie speak were inspired. It seemed the answer bloomed like a flower from River in the ground of respect. It was a river of words, in a city of "putting right."

River shared her heritage with the staff, in the midst of making food plans for all the patients and retraining their slow metabolisms. Their systems had all but shut down due of lack of food and nutrients. She had a principle of teaching healing food, with an underlying value of inter-connectedness. Somehow the minute cellular information that River understood affected all their communication.

"When one person is victimized in some way, we are all affected, we are all disrupted," Maggie said.

Gabrielle too, believed there was an order to the universe. The inter-connectedness Princess Diana had shared with them amid the gift of individuality brought in the sheaves of restoration.

There was a formidable poster on the wall of Polly's room. Hilary had pondered the mountain climber on the steep face of a cliff many times. It was a picture of endurance, but also of strength of mind. Polly had regained her individuality quicker than the others, but she also knew that repelling the cliff of grey stone was an exercise in compassion.

Jack, as he sat in the manager's office, was interested in the four points of restorative justice.

"For one, it has a focus on harms and need," he summarized. "Second, it addresses obligations. Third, it involves victims, offenders, and communities that carry out interventions. Fourth, it uses inclusive collaborative process."

"Although we are connected, we are all individuals. This is what creates our diversity," said Carla, sitting on the desk.

"Restorative justice in mental health must perform an intervention that acknowledges each person. We must be given permission to speak into their lives," said Maggie's husband.

"Justice and liberty walk hand in hand," said Gabrielle.

"Justice is composed of both interconnectedness and diversity," said Alistair.

It was Sequoia's father who had published a couple books of the poetry of Chief Dan George. J.W. Hasting had been making a name for himself both on Vancouver Island and on the mainland since the 1970's. He now offered to publish River and her column on native herbs and medicinal remedies. Most of what she had learned had come out of putting her education into practice in the most severe situations.

River's nutrition advice and education to each patient on speeding up their metabolic rate was facilitated by Maggie. Maggie had conceptualized long ago that the fear of eating and gaining weight could be assuaged by the knowledge that one day you would be at your normal thin weight and be able to eat what you wanted to. Her knowledge of human metabolism was profound. This she taught to all her patients. Maggie had every patient meet with River for a personalized and timed food plan. Each patient had a small bowl of food every two-and-a-half-hours.

After two months at City of Roses, River's case load was starting to show rapid improvement. Some of the girls were able to eat normally again, and seemed to be cured of bulimia after only one session. Jack moved River into an office on the first floor, next to the art room. Her life resonated with color.

At the staff meeting that evening, it was Jessica who thought of it first. It was an idea that had been on the back burner of their small army of fifty care workers for a few weeks now. It had begun in the night, a long time ago, as Maggie burned the candle at both ends writing *The*

Philosophy of Hunger. It had resonated in their hearts when her book was published by Simon & Schuster. Her nourishment touched hunger where death had taken her girls by the throat.

When the talking piece of a smooth blue stone reached Jessica, she brushed her dark curls from her eyes and faced the meeting. She finally said out loud what had arisen in the backs of all their minds. What evolved in their collective consciousness stirred them to dialogue. "Many First Nations initiatives have arisen in the last two years. Apologies are noted in the history of this people group. They map the shores of a civil conscience."

Carla's husband Jack agreed. "If our conscience if not based on the historical events that shape us we will not have a true voice."

Carla received the talking piece next. She paused. "Without a true voice, we may be deceived that everything is okay. My daughter is seventeen. I have recreated her over and over, to freedom, to joy, in a negative culture. Now she writes poetry too. She aligns her words on a page just as I do. I was a caring mother, but not close enough to heal the wound of my own daughter. I needed to use healing words to reach into her world," Carla said.

"She knows a word has power, and she has power over her words. She is a word-keeper, but only as a truce," said Maggie next. She passed the blue stone.

"This is the nature of the collaborative process," said Gabrielle. "We enter into the conflict, both within and without, and participate in its resolution together."

"Conflict resolution is key, I would agree," said Pat.

"The eating disordered client has unbearable conflict inside every time they eat food," said Maggie's husband.

Together as a community, they had entered into a circle of dialogue, a circle that until now had kept them out. River had admonished them to be guardians of the sacred circle, and now the shame of a generation was being amended. The blue stone passed to Alistair.

"The same human words that wound can also heal," said Alistair. "We must chose if we will use words that heal or words that kill," he said.

"The colors of words are chosen, as the paint from an artist's palette," said Eleanor, in the nature of a prelude to the fugue.

The blue stone had returned to Jessica. She pondered the prophetic nature of the smooth stone. "I have often compared the First Nations people to the nation of Israel," she said. "They are a woman who is chosen, wearing a crown like the stars of the sky."

"We are sworn to protect her. Our country stands on guard for the First Nations People," Jack said.

River received the truth of their words in a healing community that had entered her world. They had proposed an issue and dialogued a solution. It would reach into the future, as an eagle took to the sky, or a river met the sea.

"I am a nutritionist and healer," said River, "but I am only a guide. The little I know about restorative justice, I share with you." She looked at Maggie.

"When we have integrated the values of healing, compassion, and empathy into our community, we will begin to repair the torment and stigma of mental illness," said Maggie. "Thank you everyone."

 **Chapter 11**

River sat on the porch at the old homestead of J.W. Hastings, conversing over tea. It was evening, and the setting sun spun rose damask across the sky. River had spent many hours here talking with William and Evelyn. They spoke of their vision to publish and give voice to the First Nations People. They spoke of Chief Dan George, and often invited River to stay for supper.

The Hastings had four children and the dinner table was lively. River was a friend they milked for ideas on nutrition. They theorized that her book on holistic remedies would be deeply valuable to the many native bands in Canada. William walked with River around the borders of their property, to show her the horses, and the view of the countryside.

River recalled what she had written.

I open my healer's box. I take out my healer's voice. I am a healer of my people and I will not be silent anymore. My voice will rise up from the earth, as a deep spring. I will travel to the sea, to salt the shores of nations.

"Vision shines in the night," William said, as the stars came out. "The constellations guide the way. They are the map of the heavens. They speak through the distance of pain and the suffering of disease."

"The history of the stars is unchanging through the trials of humanity," said River. "When we cannot see, they light the way."

Maggie went to Portugal. It was a trip that would open possibilities for them both now and in the future. Portugal was a country that accepted Maggie with open arms; the hospital there wanted to partner with her to start another clinic. This time it would not be called City of Roses, but would be called by a new name.

When Maggie returned, she had brought Sequoia a carved wood bowl as a souvenir. It was dark and smooth, and represented to Sequoia the cups and bowls they presented to each patient. This gave the girls a sense that the food given to them in bite-sized morsels was their own.

The youngest boy, Jacob, and his care worker walked along the stone path, inviting the warm afternoon to bathe them in beauty's light. Since it was early summer, the swallows were wildly in flight against the sky and monarch butterflies paused. Hummingbirds darted here and there, in velvet red. Clare was not an imposing teacher to her young studies, but an understanding artist who saw in each patient at City of Roses their true character and worked to draw it out. Jacob's character shone clear and true. His interest in his art grew with each painting, although he was small and just learning to write words.

Clare often stood at a distance as he worked to express his emotions, wanting him to be able to regulate his own thought process. Her observations were not gratuitous. He was generous with praise for living things and sought to understand people's motives and intentions. His varied care workers imbued him with a sense of community, and that was power to young Jacob that would stand him in good stead in years to come. Where he had once bowed to anorexia in his mind and emotions, he was now steady and bold, his talents forthcoming.

The music teacher had the patients play the piano and the guitar, while Clare gave them weekly lessons in art. This opportunity was one the patients were eager for. They looked forward to their art and music lessons. Catharsis of the easel and paint, even pencil sketches, made their new-found emotions seem less frightening. The pain and even anger they felt in life had been all but been numbed by the eating disorder and starvation. As their emotions started to return, art was an indispensible tool.

Now, with the flowers in bloom, Jacob and his care worker decided to record the plants of the garden, and cut a clipping of each variety to put in a scrapbook. When they reached the stone pool, they sat for a moment on the bench. Jacob's eyes were unblinking. Carrie showed him a postcard she had received from Japan.

He fingered it carefully.

She read aloud: "Arashiyama. Togetsukyo Bridge."

He stared at the picture of the bridge shrouded in mist. It was almost translucent, so far away, yet someone had taken the picture. The bridge had been someone's muse; now it was immortal. The artist had captured his subject, and its loveliness was breathtaking.

Felicity sat by the window when Carrie and Jacob returned. They decided to make her their muse that day in art class. She was in her glory, blonde curls resplendent, shimmering in a gown of velvet with flowers in her arms for the portrait. To Clare, Felicity was truly beautiful. Yet she knew Felicity was meant for more than just the artwork of City of Roses. Felicity was elusive, a modern muse, and would be included in the filming of Gabrielle's book as a movie.

One evening, after shift, Clare ran down to the garden. The beauty of night had begun to saturate the roses, climbing the trellises of the City of Roses in fragrant blossom. They were known around Rockland for their garden. It was almost midsummer and the flowers were in full bloom. Stars appeared, winking through the thorns and arches.

Clare bent over the Albertine rose, and its perfume was intoxicating to her slender figure. With her windswept hair, she was an object of beauty as poignant as the rose garden itself. Phillip had been walking in the rose garden also. Now he reached around her and plucked the fainted bloom, stealing it like a thief after sundown. "The immortal rose," he said. She turned around. The flower still in his parched hands, he drank in the night as if travelling through a long sandy desert.

"It is the solitaire beauty," he said. "This is what will make Ebony Velvet a successful story, and film."

Clare was mesmerized by the playwright and scriptwriter. She suddenly thought, if anyone could portray Velvet in a film and have it be a success, he could. He would practically chisel a woman out of marble.

"Ebony is simple and innocent," he said. "She deserves to be understood despite her mental illness and her struggle to survive. They go hand in hand."

"I see," said Clare.

"Depicting Ebony Velvet took some time. When I see her in her own medium, and know she where she started from, I believe. I know her journey will take us to some significant places in the mind. Her framework as a writer makes her brilliant yet obscure. How could we know what she was capable of, until we mapped her thoughts like the lake shores of Hayward?"

"That is one internal landscape," Clare noted.

"The inner landscape is very much what appeals to us, as Ebony's life had more internal dialogue than external. When she talked on the inside, there was the philosopher. When she talked on the outside, we have only her poems and writings, her field journals to glean from. We know the journey she travelled was alongside many healers and healthcare professionals."

"I guess what each of them thought about the treatment of eating disorders and whether one could recover at all might be different from what we think here," Clare concluded.

"Indeed," said Phillip. "Maggie has spoken with justice into all your hearts that you can recover and live a fulfilling life."

"We'd have to believe that someone could cure anorexia, or we would not have the hope to get well," said Clare.

"It is possible that if those places Ebony lived and breathed were supposed to be healing, but turned out to be harmful... Why that might say that the doctors around her never believed she was really well. They did not believe she was cured here at City of Roses, in fact, they dared disbelieve in spite of her statistics that Maggie and her method had any credence."

"How many girls have recovered in spite of the odds? I can't imagine investing so much time and energy in people's wellness only to have others disbelieve us, take our favorite person, and drug them until they can no longer fight," said Clare.

"We must concur that there is much stigma around mental illness, and people may hurt and misunderstand Ebony in this life. They may arrest her for treatment simply because they are faced with a reality they did not know existed," he said.

"I think everyone has an inner landscape, but perhaps they are just not conscious of it. To be conscious, and know and understand what is in your subconscious mind—that takes courage beyond reckoning," said Clare.

"The person who is closest to their own subconscious mind, and the curtain has been pulled back to reveal the supernatural realm, now that is almost a dangerous combination. She walked in the spirit world, and was not one of us," he surmised.

"The spirit world talked to Ebony though. She was party to a great many revelations, and thoughts that were not of this world. Her understanding enlightened her, and she heard the voices of angels, and even the Divine."

"Clare, you are a muse, as much as Ebony. I love that about you. Your patience in the art room belies achievement."

"That is kind. Thank you Phillip," said Clare.

"May I take you to the Elephant Castle for a sample of wine after production tomorrow? Everyone around here knows you are not only an artist, but a food connoisseur," he said.

"That would be lovely," she smiled.

"I think you believe in dreams," he said.

During the months that followed, Clare continued as the art teacher at City of Roses. Jacob began to grow into an outstanding pupil and desired to please her by his paintings. When Clare walked in the rose garden, she was not alone however. As the shadows lengthened, Phillip was there also. There was an ancient love in his deep smile, and she thought it was a love of the muse. Velvet had been the object of his cultivation in filmmaking. Now he had another. It was Clare, with her long rich dark hair and brown eyes. She was a nymph of the garden, and saturated it with her kindness.

"A bud emerged in snowy steeple-white—clear as champagne was the high-bred morning," he quoted like a trill.

Chapter 12

William Hastings heard River's voice in the night, and knew it was worthy of publication. He saw her as a guide to her people, leading the way on horseback through the wilderness. He visualized the end result. Over the years he offered her a series of book contracts, and in every season she rose to the occasion.

River's writings and teachings on nutrition would deeply influence Ebony Velvet. In fact, Ebony read every word from River hungrily, looking for nourishment. It was this teaching on nutrition and health that Ebony took with her into the world. It was this and Maggie's understanding of metabolism that were questioned whenever Ebony was questioned. Was it really possible for a modern day nutritionist to believe that calories don't count? Could they say with conviction that a patient should only be weighed backwards?

Ebony would live, holding her breath, that River's principles of restorative justice would be an asset to society. She bit her lip over whether it would be accepted among mental health professionals to have a restorative option to staid medical orthodoxy. If Ebony was unlike a bridge, River flowed beneath her. She gave Ebony purpose and direction.

It was not long after Jack had hired a new care worker, Erin, that the office on the first floor was witness to an argument. The new care worker was in a disagreement with Jack. She wanted a raise, and a promotion, but Jack did not agree. Since she was their newest employee, her request seemed almost brazen.

The argument started again the next afternoon in the attic. As Carla held the spoon to little Avery's mouth, Erin—who was with another patient across the room— erupted.

"What are you doing?" she said. "If Avery wants to eat she'll eat on her own."

Carla dropped the spoon in surprise. The girls looked bewildered at the outburst.

"You were shoving the spoon right down her throat," Erin insisted.

"This is the way we do it here, at the outset," said Carla.

"Avery doesn't want to eat, though," said Erin, in her cold journalist voice. "You're force-feeding her."

"Erin," Carla dropped her voice. "If you disagree that the weakest of us need to be spoon fed, you'll need to talk to Jack downstairs." Erin resented her authority, she could tell.

"Wait a minute," she said as she paged Jack, praying, "Please answer..."

Jack paged back to instruct Carla to look after both girls, and asked her to send Erin down to the office.

When Erin stuck her head in the manager's office where Jack was working, she was not happy. How dare they humiliate young girls with a diet of whole foods, she seethed inwardly. On the outside she was a cool as a cucumber.

Jack was calm but loyal to the clinic. "Erin," he said, "We can't have disputes on the second and third floor over food. This is not an appropriate response, particularly coming from a new worker."

"You don't know what happened," Erin said.

"If you really don't agree with Carla, I may have to let you go," said Jack diplomatically.

Erin turned and stormed out of the lobby, down the red stairs, and left in a cloud of exhaust.

It seemed to Jack, on reflection and talking to Carla later, that Erin saw too many sides to every argument. She did not interpret their protocol as compassion; she almost sided with the condition. The next day, he mentioned the incident to Maggie. The director was distracted and hardly seemed to notice. Little did they suspect that Erin, who had been a journalist, would take a job at the newspaper and the backlash against them would begin.

It was swift but cruel when they received the notice of a court order to close City of Roses. They were being taken to court. The media frenzy that followed was as if there were sharks in the waters. Maggie could not brush this away like a strand of her white-blonde curls. Her large dark eyes showed pain. For the first time she considered that they were up against something that was deathly and made them afraid. Was it the third mansion, the mansion of forgotten love, that threatened to swallow the hard work and dedication of City of Roses? Would someone really insist in a court of law that her patients would be better off in a psych ward?

The care workers were silent. Sequoia could not fathom the many newspaper headlines, the insults, the implied and overt misunderstanding of their intentions. Jessica, their lawyer who was asked to represent them, was the only one who dared face the challenge, as she had every day with her pride intact—head held high, she constructed her defense. She would make her case. Inwardly she was holding her breath. Had she once written, *"Calm are the waves offshore"*?

The retribution was furious. First there were articles from the Times, then the Province and Sun. They questioned Maggie's motives from every angle. They derided her for not having a doctorate, and then called her an amateur. They tried to piece together a story of the clinic and its opponents, its patients and their parents, but the story was cut into such small pieces that it was no longer palatable.

One of the reporters began writing a book to discredit them. After the publicity Maggie had received with Oprah Winfrey, there were a thousand people on their waiting list. Oprah had publicly praised Maggie and called her an angel. Now the most derogatory of reporters was trumpeting, "Fallen Angel."

They would have their day in court. City of Roses summoned those who would stand as witnesses. Any of the graduates of City of Roses were invited to testify of the positive outcome of the program. Jack and Carla agreed that the court case was paramount. It could no longer be avoided that Maggie's method had cured hundreds of young men and women. They deserved to win, and had little doubt as to the outcome.

Jessica, in her winning and charismatic representation of the clinic, was probably the most disappointed when they lost. In December of 1999 the British Columbia government closed down the clinic citing that Maggie and the clinic staff "physically restrained patients, force fed, verbally threatened and mentally abused them." The closure of the clinic made headlines across Canada.

Contemplations of Revelation

O true River,
O true waters flowing down,
O true legends of the deep,
O spirit of the mountain to the sea,
Sweep on!

O only four directions
of the four medicines,
(from innocence to strength)
It is the wind that moves the trees!

O waterhouse of all earth's unseen springs,
O portrait of the skies' bright indigo bead,
It is the earring of the Great Spirit!

O Visions of the tribal dance,
O Sweep of sunlight's fiery chance,
O Moon's sonata, rising true,
O Community that caused the wound,
O You shall heal it too,
Lamp to the darkness!

Part IV: Dying Swan

Chapter 13

It was not long after the filming at City of Roses that Rose returned to Bavaria. Her husband met her at the airport in Germany. Her little family was happy to have her return, under the eaves of their cottage with a garden. She looked out the window, and saw the New Swan Stone Castle's white turrets off in the distance. So much time had passed, and so many things had happened since she had last been here. A stork flew by. Oliver sat at the table, doing his sums.

"Hello," she called.

"Mom!" he enclosed her in a hug.

She had much to tell them, and it kept them enthralled long into the night. There were the methods of testing theory, and the legends of the deep, but Rose belonged to both. What she now knew of the four directions, of the wind that would blow from the north, had affected her health and her reason. Both art and science led her now, both poetry and practicality.

The next day Rose read the letters that had arrived in her absence from her friend, Galina Sarnova. Galina was a dancer for the Bolshoi, and also suffered from an eating disorder. She had met Rose while vacationing in Europe once and they remained close friends.

October 12, 1999

Dear Rose,

When I met with the sea of faces at the station, I was wearing three sets of clothes, as I had been instructed by my mother. I was carrying my carpet bag, with only clothing and my journal and pen from my personal life. All other items that had once marked me, Galina, as an individual had been left behind. I was a dancer for the Bolshoi Ballet now, and only two nights before had said goodbye to all my friends at a small gathering in our living room. I was headed for Moscow, and the big city beckoned, as did the upcoming Swan Lake, for which I would be auditioning.

It was only four months before that I had been recruited by the ballet in my hometown of Reutov. The stale summer air had waited placidly outside as I and four other dancers had stood in line, waiting for our turn to perform what we had each rehearsed for over nine months. In the end, it was I, Galina Sarnova, who was chosen at just sixteen, to continue my young life in Moscow as a ballerina for the Bolshoi. It was 1995 and this is what I had dreamed of all my life, and now my dream was finally a reality.

As I boarded the train, I looked ahead, following the line of dark-haired passengers. Finding my seat, I put my bag overhead, and leaned to peer out the window through the dim lights of November. My mother and father waved goodbye as I left, the first Jew in our town to become a successful dancer. My training had given me a steel heart: when I was most lithe and delicate, I was most strong. But would I pay the price?

I remembered my father, Andrei, the librarian in our town, as I had always known him—sunlight slanting through dusty stacks of old books, shelving, categorizing, and reading. Always with a book in hand, he had taught me a love of literature along with the ballet. A frequent traveler, he had many times made the trip to Moscow to acquire old books for the library collection. My mother, Yulia, on the other hand, had raised three children: I and my two brothers, Anton and Mikhail. She was a violinist who did solo performances and played with the orchestra. When twilight descended on our town, if one leaned out the window far enough, one could hear the sweet strains of the violin, lingering over the roofs.

It was my mother who had encouraged me to dance, taken me the ballet master's class, and bought me my first set of toe shoes. My mother had taken the little extra money we had, and paid for my dance lessons since I was four. Although my grandparents were well off, and lived in the same town, it was my parents' frugal intentions of always putting the dance first that had bought my ticket to Moscow at fourteen. And just as my earliest memory of the dance was etched in my mind, the first plié, the painful turnout, so that day would be forever in my memory, when I boarded the train for Moscow.

Love, Galina

November 15, 1999

Dear Rose,

The countryside rumbled by in patchwork progression, a continuum of noise and distance. As my new home approached, where I would live in a rooming house with other dancers, I realized my life had taken a turn for the better. I thought it would be in my best interest to hold my head high, be as proud as a dancer was for the Bolshoi, and never admit defeat. Somehow, in the right combination, I would put together the ingredients that would mean success for more than just myself, but for everyone I touched with the gift of dance and for the company I represented. I was compelled to dance, and to be lost completely in the meld of dancers that formed the corps de ballet. Day after day, with unceasing inspiration, I was to win over everything inside me that wanted to dance and forget everything else about my life. Even as perspiration dripped from my brow, as I worked out the movements hour after hour, my fragile form grew strong from ballet.

Ballet was like a seamstress, hemming my form-flattering garment from neck to foot. Even as I stretched and raised en Pointe, she sewed, never-tiring of making a librarian's daughter into a beauty. My neck was always turned just so, my head tilted, and my arms a perfect round. To the barre, from first position onward—the excitement of being a new girl in Moscow had leisurely turned to polished professionalism. Many of the other dancers would put on airs, but under the façade, I began to see that really it was a cover for the years of pain and hard work of the tireless look of dance. For it was not generally known, that after years of dance, one's feet began to blacken and harden, always kept under cover, never shown to anyone outside the ballet, as they were the instruments of each movement, and no one must ever guess the cost.

Love, Galina

December 21, 1999

Dear Rose,

December passed, with its cruel freezing snow drifts; and with a week off at Christmas I had returned home to my village on the outskirts of Moscow. The oranges, nuts, and chocolates had been an indulgent mistake, however, as I needed to be as stringent as possible to compete with the other dancers for the most coveted parts. Returning the beginning of January, I realized I was unable to hide even an extra five pounds beneath my leotard, and so began to exercise strenuously after hours to regain my shape. At last, in late February the audition for Swan Lake arrived, and we lined up beside the piano to wait our turn in front of the directors. My hair was pinned tightly into a bun, my toe shoe ribbons neatly sewed, and my leotard was taunt. The music began.

I lurched forward En pointe with the other dancers in my group, and then I almost closed my eyes, for I knew the movements off by heart. I let the music carry me, until I became the swan, until I could no longer ever return and just be me, Galina. The world spun in some hazy dream, until the ballet master tapped his cane, and motioned us off right. "Next," he said, and the next group of dancers appeared.

I walked home after the audition. It had begun to rain, and the snow was beginning to melt. The sky was grey, and my legs were sore and almost buckled under me. I had practiced all these months for the part, but what if it eluded me, and I did not make the corps of Swan Lake? All the rhyme and reason of hard work, culminating in the one austere moment of acceptance or rejection were beginning to dawn on me in the life of a dancer. I knew I must become more regular and less home-spun. The practicalities of life must tone my personality until I was not feeble in my attempts to perform, but seasoned and expected, wanted and demanded of.

Something about my mannerisms changed that day. My toes turned out on their own, my long hair drawn up, my face gaunt, my fingers rested in thin air. As I waited to hear the results of the audition, I became steady, level-headed, and practical in how I would go about my career. I would never let another dancer get the better of me. I, Galina, was determined to play any part I auditioned for and carry it through with just determination and perseverance.

Not only that, but something about my large eyes and heady smile, with a slight pout, was beginning to win over the directors among the most competitive of my colleagues. I had made the corps de ballet of the Bolshoi on the first audition, along with almost 80 other dancers. Now I wanted to dance in Swan Lake.

Love, Galina

January 17, 2000

Dear Rose,

Our schedule for Swan Lake went on, rigorously demanding, practicing for six hours a day. I examined my figure from every angle, admiring its new graces, imagining myself on stage, and wanting more than anything to prove that the discipline I had now would stay with me for the length of my career as a dancer. Sure, I had practiced hard, and the ballet had been my training for over a decade now, but the other dancers were older and more experienced. I learned everything I could just from watching them: dance, dance, repetition, repetition, until the sweat dripped from my brow and I could no longer stand up.

"Galina," Anastasia said, admiringly, "you are a natural."

"Movements should be effortless," said the ballet master.

The piano began again and we gilded the wall, standing on one foot like birds.

There was something enamoring about seeing the corps de ballet as one entity, moving always in unison, the flutter of crinolines. With the seasoned grace of only a true athlete, we knew that both our competition and our unity made us proud. We were the finest in Russia, and on opening night, all of Moscow would see its celebrated young dancers in top form.

Andrei, my father, came to visit the Bolshoi for Swan Lake. I took his arm and thanked him, and he gave me a single red rose before the performance and wished me good luck. My tutu was made of mesh and feathers, and somehow on opening night, and every performance thereafter, we became light as angels, and bright as stars. The music sounded from the orchestra pit, and *now there was no ballet director at the front of the room, no out-of-tune piano dictating an arabesque, no sweaty leotards, or worn ribbons. Our hair was pasted black against our heads with hair glue, our faces white with powder. Only the demarcations in the wood floor belayed the long hours of practice, and now Swan Lake had begun.*

Love, Galina

 **Chapter 14**

Rose continued to read Galina's small pile of letters, eloquently penned from Moscow.

The next one was dated February 19, 2000.

Dear Rose,

My father watched every season performance while I danced in the Bolshoi. If there was one thing I know, it is that the son of a wealthy lawyer, who was the chief connoisseur of fine books in the small town of Reutov, would never miss a chance to see his first-born in the ballet over the next four years. Somehow he knew this chance was one he would treasure for his short lifetime, and that the days of dance could abruptly come to a close at the onset as a disease like anorexia. He traveled to Moscow quite frequently on the guise of business.

I, Galina, did not forget to return home, to see my two brothers Anton and Mikhail, who were growing up quickly while attending the village school. My mother missed me the most, and her favorite, a pot of Borscht simmering on the stove, was what I expected with a loaf of Russian brown bread. We sat around the table at sundown, and did not neglect to celebrate the Passover meal. For we were Russian Jews, and lit our

candles with each Friday dinner so as not to forget our sins and
our faith in God.

God had sustained us through the centuries, admonishing our
minds to the study of the Scriptures, arising as rudimentary in
the day to day provision of the work of our hands, a threnody
through every crisis and dilemma, and his manifestation told us
to heed his presence. I knew the staunch and stoic faith of the
Jews was rising in amendment to worldly hatred and violence.
My attenuation was chaste and accomplished, for I had
promised the God of the Jews, with rapture and beguiled soul to
preserve the treasure of my heart. He had not refused me.

Love, Galina

March 10, 2000

Dear Rose,

The commission was upon us to do our duty to our fellow
man, not only to always work to the best of our ability, but to
light our candles each night with the blessing that comes from a
soul that has derived hope from the unknown and the unseen,
that has harnessed the power of that which is invisible to act on
its behalf. The reverberation of the violin throughout our
immaculate home had always taught us that the practical was
juxtaposed with the transcendent. Now we took hands to pray
this Sabbath.

"Galina, you are perplexed with the remarkable emotion and
its weight that carries you though each performance; yet it is
God who has purposed to act in this way around you. Let us ask
him for his special blessing to preserve you though all that lies

ahead, that you may not falter in his purpose for your life. He will not ignore your prayers, but will deliver you."

"Thank you, Father," I said.

My mother added, "The way of your life has been engraved upon your conscience, like an emblem you wear of what you have welcomed even without comprehension. Your oratory of the sacred is not incomplete, and the world will not deceive you into false flattery."

My two brothers both sanctioned my parents' words by nodding their heads. They knew something important was occurring, and that my parents, like many others, could see into a future that had yet to unfold with penetrating depth and accuracy. The future of our people would include prohibitions too great for us to conceptualize, but it was my father's well-read rhetoric, his mentorship of books that formed the words in my mind even before I had the opportunity to put them to paper.

Love, Galina

April 14, 2000

Dear Rose,

My Eating Disorder Emissary—by the wind of night, compensate suffering and arise from the disorder of anorexia, to enlist followers for their liberation.

What was the disorder and chaos into which we would fall at the hands of torturers, the suffering that had seemingly no solace, the dark night of no return of anorexia. I knew even as I left my parents' home in Reutov and returned to the Bolshoi, that I would continue on, unchained, to endear and captivate my audience with raptures of the ballet. It was January again.

The sky was like frosted glass and cold over Moscow's inner circle. When I came inside, the other girls surrounded me and took off my coat and my mittens, they brought me into the parlor where we stood around the fire and traded tales, with hot mugs of tea. There was a sovereign touch that swayed us on command, as the wind in a field, when on a stage. We were the corps, and our words danced as our thoughts, ornaments of a greater empire of the vast land of snow and ice.

Finally, it came time to go to bed, and we reluctantly parted, back into the rooms where we hung our slippers on the backs of our doors, coaxed our freshly washed leotards into submission for another season, and prayed on our knees for God to bless us and make us beautified for the dance. There was always the competitive edge of stardom, and in contrast the softening emollient of our elusiveness. There was an accent that fell on the behaviors that would further our careers, and a trepidation around all other activities. I found life outside the dance was curtailed to the pages of my journal, where I wrote as if one impoverished of words, the summary of how bravery shone above cowardice when we put the renown of the ballet above our own.

May I never fall into dross, I thought, as I stoked the cinders of my fire. For the work of anything besides the dance was like that of a drudge to me; I could not plod on like a domesticated animal when the overcast sovereignty had, to my duress, posed me articulate and dulcet. I was always decorously in continuance of a long tradition. And I was in allegiance to only God, always cordial of my country.

How did my story come about: there was the flight of a bird, the swift descent and ascension, and then the disappearing into the invisible. There was the hovering of evening solstice, and the dying of any wind. There was the disappearing of the last rays of the sun into night.

Love, Galina

May 15, 2000

Dear Rose,

The parlance of the locals was like the patter of rain into the imperceptible dust, as they watched me, the young dancer gain a foothold under the pressures of rehearsal and performance. I strode with determination into each audition now, every new ballet a guise for the classic script, having resolved to find my limitations mixed with strength.

My father's prominence and distinction made him a public figure with empyrean tastes, the sublimated collection he strove to acquire, began to make its exodus into Moscow for safe keeping from libraries and collection across Europe. Book by book joined its illustrious position in the collection of Reutov, even some from the unknown underground of Moscow's art world.

I had been brought up in a hard working social class, but it was one with money, where my mother was a musician, and a fine one. Her vocation was always an inspiration, and now as the Russian winter threatened to deplete our senses, causing us to huddle under the covers for warmth, I longed for the sound of her violin, the comforting touch of her hand. She had warned me that to want anything besides what I had was frivolous, and knew I would never become vain and exhausted. I was making a small stipend, which I sent home to them for safe keeping. The glory of my ballet days was a lament to the refinement of my symmetry, and the call "to the barre" was dirgeful, mournful, and plaintive.

Love, Galina

June 25, 2000

Dear Rose,

Mine was a familiar weakness. I was prone to compromise like a bird was made for flight. It was stable, endearing, and uncomplicated. I never used force on my body but collaborated with every ideal. The ballet was a force in motion, however, taming the savagery of my wild beauty into gentility. Every day was a painful reminder that dance as a career was not for the whimsical and foolish, but those with notions of strategy, competition and cadence.

My elevation was a departure from loftiness into humility. I was a character in each dance that held a distinctness that had to do with frugality, husbandry, and providence over the frenzy and trance of selfishness. My old ways had left me forever for the new makeup, the glitz of lights, the portent stage, the formality of curtseys and tutus.

For enmity or love, I imagined a better world in the darkness without anorexia to mar my world, and Moscow was a dancer with black toe shoes and a beating heart. I saw in my mind's eye the first arabesque, and as I walked every day to the Bolshoi to dance, I began to notice the city beginning to change. Anorexia reminded me of how Hitler had taken over Russia, along with the rest of Europe, and although Moscow remained free, the cities and towns surrounding were once in the throes of the occupation. The soldiers had made it difficult if not impossible to leave the city to travel home. The furious circle of force and terror. Will I ever be well?

Love, Galina

July 1, 2000

Dear Rose,

The ballet commanded our adept and skillful dexterity, while to any departure from the norm, we turned our heads, very resolutely in pious and grave ignorance. With saintly passion, we chose our steps, ignoring the indigence and privation allotted to the students under eighty pounds.

Anorexia's infernal hold was a confinement with restraint ordered for every dancer under the necessary weight, and while the psych ward of the Moscow hospital took over for some, my body was not exempt. The particulars were not to be known to me until much later, but with minute precision I would find them out, and then regulate my answer to the controlling and malevolent force that had overtaken me. All in the name of help and concern, I was kept in the psych ward for two weeks. It was while I was still in the ballet that I began to bargain with death,

even as I loved, trading all my concentrated effort and energy to
defeat its mortal grip.

Love had always been for me the only force against death
and anorexia, and my love was young, strong, and guileless.
Surely the ocean that surrounded me would not sweep me away.
I was resolute at the confidence that the journey's fragrant
chord had asked of me. It asked of me my very soul; the faint
celestial heights. I knew my spirit yearned for this paradise.
                                        Love, Galina

It was on reading Galina's last letter, that Rose realized
the truth. Galina had written her over the past ten
months to tell her of her struggle to live while suffering
from anorexia; but she had not survived. Rose's husband
Friedrich gently told her that Galina had died of the
condition only a week before. Rose bowed her head.
Galina had been a dying swan, and Rose had not noticed
her anguish. Swan Lake would go on, but now without
Galina. The Bolshoi was a prima ballerina under the
bright lights. She bent with purpose, always waiting for
the next arabesque, and resounded, dying, before the
applause.

Contemplations of Revelation

O true Father,
O true provider,
O true guidance,
O spirit of protection,
Teach!

O parental soul
of the child in three dimensions,
(mind, body, spirit)
Encircle!

O leader of the family home,
O covenant partner of the sacred union,
Love!

O Restorer of the cell of procreation,
O Reassurance of the universe's ordering of life,
O Strong tower, be a place of refuge
O City on a hill, now lighthouse to the ocean's roar,
O Fortress of ongoing safety amid strife,
Unify!

Part V: Muse In A White Gown

 **Chapter 15**

The tiny soul quavered, a solitary figure in white—captive with inner purity. The small but beating heart, translucent, free only to look out at the world beyond, from behind a door that was firmly closed to reason—was without any further cause than to rend the world for its purposes. She stared at a closed door in a hospital psych ward, while her dark auburn hair streamed down her back.

Ebony Velvet was not fearful of anyone—but small, cold, and livid for a long time. Perhaps she had lived in a house with only a fire for heat, and when the wood ran out, the cold seeped through the floors and chilled the very core of her person. She did not believe in being poor. She was rich in a world far beyond this one. She collected the gems of the natural world, and called them forth in settings of fire.

Where the cherry trees touch dusk in descant—
wine branches blossom effulgent, white,
all darkness of the night for this full time—
I wander 'neath the fading light, recant.
Seasons of my soul were like a grand home

I sojourned in once, for the staid calling
when all life pauses before the falling.

The invalid was destined to find none
of the aforementioned illness beneath
these eaves of healthy grandeur, sunlight near
the slant of shadows, refracted prism tear
that moved over the house, the sea, the heath.
If I, in fury, could my earth restrain,
I would a hundred blossoms in my train.

It was a sonnet she had written, that she thought of now. When only an infant, Ebony had fallen down the basement stairs to the cement at the bottom. Her parents, the Velvets, had taken her to the hospital for observation. Was this her first stay in a psych ward? When she was four, although still a child, she had spoken into many situations with a sureness.

The fire was a sureness of the presence of love, and the initiative deep within her tiny soul to find it. It burned as the warmth of cloves in cider, or a pungent desire for spiritual fervor. Something deeper than distain for neglect made us rise as the sun in the morning, and retire with the darkness of night. Something beyond the avoidance of abuse made us behave kindly to others; for love cannot be silenced. This very force made Ebony into a mother when she least expected it, and her child was Snowflake Princess.

The earth, who was caretaker, was both her mother and her father. The principalities over love and nature were as old as the universe. They took her alongside, and measured out her emotions. There were the angels over seas, lands, moons, and constellations and they bowed to the Divine.

The metal was a door closing in her mind that seemed to never open again; it was the kindness to detain your violence. There were the young broken women who came in and out, and the ones who would stay forever. Was this the only place that was safe from the abusive spouses and boyfriends which caused them to fly in the night? This seemed the case if you thought you were battered because you were bad, while believing the best of everyone else. Love flies.

In the psych ward, even young children could visit, but now they were held in the arms of others who loved them. Someone was having a birthday. It was Elle's one year old daughter. They served her red velvet cake. She blew out her silver candle. Elle was smart and beautiful, but she had done drugs in front of a child. Now someone else took care of her daughter, while she endured group therapy and narcotics anonymous.

The water was falling over and over again in hysterical notions of what is acceptable. When people got it wrong, they had to start all over again. After several years, you might get your child back. In the meantime you might have to work part-time at the supermarket.

The wood was the walls of the interfaith chapel downstairs. There were panels that said "Believe" in red velour. Ebony wished she could sit in the pew and just

rest her head awhile, but it was off limits. The Chaplain
came and prayed by their bedsides, but only if you
requested it.

"I am founding the Immaculate Conception Church,"
she said.

"Is this a new religion?" asked the Chaplain.

"It is a church that encompasses all religions and all
denominations," she replied casually.

"How did this come about?" he asked. "I am
interested."

"I think the unity of true believers will stem from a
prophecy, given by a dark child in chains. Perhaps it will
be a book of a thousand pages, anointed as the last words
to a lost generation."

"Is that dark child you?" he asked.

"I am its author," she answered.

"But you must know that prophecy is a common form
of speech nowadays. In just about every charismatic
church they believe in this gift," said the Chaplain.

"True," Ebony replied, "but I am Roman Catholic.
That is how I was raised."

This was far out on a limb for a Roman Catholic to
believe in the gifts of the spirit to be practiced in such a
way, the Chaplain thought. Ebony might as well have
thrown the church doors wide open.

"I think that prophecy has overflowed the bounds of
the church, and quite literally seeped onto the streets
where it is practiced by everyone who desires to
strengthen and encourage," she only said.

"What a thought! You are going places, I can tell. For who would receive a prophetic word from anyone on the street instead of a trusted few prophets, until just this moment," he answered.

"Thank you," she said.

"I would like to look at this website, of the Immaculate Conception Church," he said.

Ebony took a pen out of the drawer and wrote it down for him. It was apparent to him that she was both a writer and a visionary. But her prophetic journey had come from being a people watcher. She had spent her life, since four years old, sitting on a curb—watching the world go by.

Ebony wrote in her journal of the encounter with the Chaplain. She could never be an observer without careful notes. She would never be a candid writer without discretion. If she desired to write, it would only be as accurate as the age markings of a tree, rings of knowledge dispersed over time.

Who was it that found her a sight for sore eyes? Who loved her more than the objects of their affection? This love was forbidden. When she loved, was it a rejection of the selfless church, the element of martyrdom?

Ebony sat in the hospital, an involuntary patient—a forced martyr with a bitter remedy. An orderly entered, and placed several packs of cigarettes on her roommate's bedside table. She turned her head in ignorance. She closed her eyes in guilt. Her medication was placed in a small paper cup beside the bed. But she refused.

The orderlies were called. They dragged her down the hallway to the seclusion room. She screamed in terror. She did not want to be injected up with drugs until she passed out. She was left in the isolating darkness on the cold floor. She thought, "They take away your clothing. They leave you alone in your stupor. You are far away from everyone and everything that hurt you, they think. That is what you wanted, or you would comply."

"The arrows in your soul were flaming with pain not your own, and spirit eyes—green and gold, grew dull with the blaming of cold transgressions. Like woven dyes, peppering the wool with old colors youthful rebellion could not temper and sacred conscience not remember," said the orderly.

Ebony was all alone in the world. Here, all doors were closed to her, and love was gone. The windows of her soul were all darkened. It was here, in the torture of all that loves, in the dead of night she sang: one voice rose that rang true. On and on into the darkness she travelled. She did not know when she would reach her destination, all she knew was that at that moment heaven or hell became a personal decision that she alone could make. Like a passenger on a train that rattled on and on, she waited on the Divine's doorstep.

Chapter 16

The bride was a woman in white, with a hundred blossoms in her train; and so also, the patient in a hospital gown grows white with demineralization. The woman of one love flourishes as a blossoming tree, secure within her household. The psych ward patient waits for an unrealized opportunity and the resources she needs are faintly beyond her. Ebony would languish in utter rejection of the heart, or find a way to love innocence.

The nurse took her out of the seclusion room.

"When joy of life outweighs its sorrow, you will find the quiet touch of night: the reunion of the bright morrow of bliss incarnate without respite, and all that lingers of suffering—only a faint memory, etching itself in this character of thine," she said to herself.

Ebony could not stand up. She fainted and hit her head on the sink board. The nurse caught her, but the incident left a bruise on her forehead. She could not even lift the spoon to her mouth after being in the seclusion room. She had to be spoon-fed at every meal. Mrs. Velvet was well-to-do, and ignored this ill-treatment of her daughter.

Ebony knelt beside her bed a week later. With no other options, and no way out, she prayed, "Lead the way through the wilderness. Take me to drink at the coldest stream. Lambs in a pasture, lying in the heather, bleat in their rest, under the shadow of a presence. Leaning into the future, someone runs from the past where there is no purpose. And the time for laughter is etched in heaven, like sorrow is engraved in your palms.

"Eternal youth has a wanting, looking over a woman's shoulder into the distance. Taking hold of the old dreams where death lingers, and building a home. The hearth is a place where a heart warms to the rhythm of your drum, pounding, lost in your dark eyes. And you take hands— for a lifetime of affection and romance."

The secret apple tree seemed to scorn its rule, the fruit of its branches an utter rejection of the maker. The forbidden fruit was to know one's own evil, instead of one's innocence. This is what she had realized. Ebony believed there was only one missing scripture, and it was "Be ye innocent, for I am innocent."

The woman in white redeemed herself by writing behind closed doors—but there was the cooking and cleaning, pruning and gardening, baking and sewing. She was a domesticated servant of her duty, and passion was forbidden. Yet what is life without desire? What is love without children? Only meters away, a pulsating blood-red pomegranate hung from the loamy green of the Tree of Life, separated on the inside into individual cells.

Ebony wrote, in longhand:

I cannot work but linger in the field. Thus cannot eat, but walk upon the hills. He is the facet of my trumpet pealed. His labor drives the water from its fill. O mortal wound, upon this silent hour! I cannot slay me, I am overcome. The thirst be quenched and speaking of its power, in this game where only I am won. He works, he toils, he sweats beneath the sun. And I will write what nature has begun: epiphany in me dwells to be sung—for I am lonely, misfit, barren one. What of my woeful rights do I procure, to stand and now demand my life mature?

When observing the day, she noticed that the cultivated garden outside reaped its metered hedge and manicured lawns, the lily, the rose "*Shade of Pale,*" and spirited marigold. Yet the wild wood has stood since the inception of time, she thought. The California redwoods tower as tall stately film goddesses on the red carpet. The rain forests of Vancouver Island were coveted canopy, and coastal Douglas firs protected species.

She noted:

The poplar grove bloomed in catkins, with rough bark and white cottony seeds. The sun did not hasten to its wooded floor. The stars barely whispered below its lattice. And humankind

stopped at its brow, plunged its neck into the dark respite, and
gave a thorough holler oft the branches, made its gates a barred
fairy haunt.

Spirits unknown lived within these trees, spoke in lavish
darkling speech. Rumored in their feathery leaves, marked their
white bark with black remark. How to transcend, while seated
beneath this poplar rising spire from earth to heaven? The
gratuities of life cannot in fullness pay that vein which runs
beneath with blood.

All the natural medicine Ebony had experienced in her
lifetime was a bounty she would not neglect to harvest.
She did not forget to eat the food of her small organic
garden at home, with its sweet potatoes, yams, and
spindly beans. She saw it now as a holistic attempt at
integration, mining the world of health from the
perspective of her own poverty. For was it not vitamins
she craved—isolated, sterilized, in bottles in the health
food store; it was herbs that soothed—bottled and bagged
for teas, tinctures, emulsions, and infusions. When she
was at home, she drank seven cups of herbal tea a day
made from spring water.

The earth was deep beneath her, yet it refused to
accept the roots of her tree. Try as she might, she could
not root herself in the community. She had dabbled in the
arts, and had studied Botany at university. The Velvets
had valued education and given their daughter her choice

of ivy-league schools. Her grandmother had insisted she take music lessons throughout her childhood.

"Only the best for Ebony," she would attest at every birthday with a special gift.

Yet, Ebony had been diagnosed with more than one disease as an adult. She had known regret instead of forgiveness. The words she had heard spoken were not nurturing and kind, but a refusal to accept her. She wished to disappear, as she wished to renounce all the symptoms of her illness. Yet she existed, and her very existence was horror. It discarded her honor. It shattered her beliefs in the seeds of what she thought would grow into something reputable.

When she had nothing left to lose, Ebony would be a catalyst for change. She would see that she was unhappy with the status quo. She would refuse to comply with what failed her. She would insist that things be different. If she could not change others, she would suffer—because they would try to change her instead.

The doctor saw Ebony every morning at eight.

"Stop fearing yourself," he said. "You are more capable than you know."

"How can I do so when I must lie in utter paralysis that my future is grim?" she asked.

"Why not try to be more successful. Your attempts have failed until now," he answered.

"What should I do?" she asked, feeling a thorn of self-pity.

"You must always specialize in life, so you do something in the world that no one else can. No one else will ever accomplish what you alone do in your lifetime."

Her dark eyelashes blinked. Her face was naked. She did not even have makeup privileges. She did not have her own clothing either, for that matter, only a hospital gown and bathrobe.

She lay still for hours on end. Her arms were stretched out. She mentally recited the stations of the cross; for six hours she lay without moving. There was no blinking of eyes—she was still and in a trance.

"The pore of the natural earth opened and from it came a bundle of lavender, steaming and purple—its buoyant perfume was a postcard from beneath the ground. The practice of harvesting herbs came from a long tradition, handed down from generation to generation, to know of each wild grass and flower, its time and season. Such a conscientious act, to pluck each species at its brightest, plunge its fiery aroma into an oil above the flame, imbue from it a fragrant rain," she thought.

Ebony stood in the field, and the flowers stretched for as far as the eye could see: a populace of royalty's test, riveted by her rich black earthen tea. Her mind was finally still. She knew clearly who she was. "I am all alone in the world," she said. There was an utter rejection. To be wanted by someone, to be needed, that was the only thing she had thought of as normative. She thought she had something to offer society, yet felt restrained to a bed.

"That is not a good way to control your emotions. You will lose your mobility if you do that," the psychiatrist said. "I am recommending you to physiotherapy."

"Yes," she replied. "I'll do physio."

She was willing to do the exercises. She was not averse to stretches on the mats in various lotus poses, with music overhead. She did not want to lose her mobility, for she knew she had osteoporosis—she had been diagnosed with the brittle disease at twenty-three.

Chapter 17

The psychiatrist spoke into the silence.

"How are you doing this morning?" he asked, as he did every day.

"Fine," Ebony insisted.

"But how is your mood?" he questioned further.

She noted internally that this seemed his favorite question, and since she was an introvert, when she was stressed she never let it show. She preferred to spend most of her time alone, and resented his assumptions. Even more, the hospital invaded her quiet time with a sterile preoccupation. The only distraction she had was a small transistor radio that received her favorite station.

People had commended her for her tolerance to stress on many occasions, for she never lost her cool. She would not lose it now. Here, she was only one hundred pounds, but she had always been petite. She had been taught how to eat properly at City of Roses. She did not believe she still had anorexia.

The psychiatrist thought differently. He had her weighed by the nurse every day, and they took her blood pressure and temperature. They encouraged her to eat and gain weight. The nurse came by every night with a small paper cup containing her medication. She had no option but to swallow it down with water.

"With any disease or condition there are many emotions attached to both sickness and wellness. We feel guilt when those we love suffer unnecessarily. To have that guilt continue for many years erodes the fabric of relationship and health in those around mental illness sufferers. Some of these children have tragically died from the condition, etching the guilt into lines of grief," the psychiatrist said.

Ebony sat in the chair across from his desk. The nightingale flew in Ebony's mind. The bird was not brittle anymore. The bird disappeared under the rain, where the dark clouds were rimmed with last gold. The nightingale was trading all her failures for flight and song. He was not afraid of the real or the surreal; the symbol of his existence was appearing and disappearing. For Ebony that was knowing when the dance took you off right, and when you were center stage.

"When there is nothing that can be done to cure a disease or to save a dying child, the pain is very deep in a parent's soul. Now we have anti-psychotic drugs. At least you can expect not to spend your life in a psych ward. We now very effectively integrate psych patients back into the community. Even if you have waited a long time to hear these words, I would exhort you not to give up right now," he said.

"Hyacinth, handcuffed to a dying field, the guileful cold. Bereft shadow grafted—the furrows of yesteryear, fringing yield. The exile of vegetables: the drafted two-tone harvest on cue, the dreamy corn. The chestnut lookout, with buckeye about, appraise the rusty treasure amid thorn," Ebony thought.

She heard his words, but she had never been suicidal. She could not fathom spending the rest of her life dependent on medication—so she would not respond. This was only a method of medicine that employed force, not conflict resolution. It demanded compliance not collaboration. If she had been asked for her cooperation in the first place, she might have been able to choose to heal. She was not given that option—to be a voluntary patient—and internally she felt the horror. She walked back along the corridor.

Ebony very definitively put on her ballet shoes in the exercise room in the dark. Then, with one grand jeté, she danced upon it on the hardwood floor. That is how she had been taught to deal with injustice. Her very body released its tensions, the unforgiveness melted beneath her feet. Her doleful smile emanated like the plaintive movement in trees from sapwood to heartwood. Rueful at this great live bulwark moving in the wind, right and left, with poignant pinecones touching ground.

Her thesis would at last cross this earth on last slanted sunlight, over the shadowed path. When kindness would rule as a queen, the night would be star-thick, spelling joy from one generation to the next. In this time, overcome, she wrote in her field journal.

The dance was something choreographed and predictable. It was deeply physical, and intrinsically spiritual. It captured you and set you free. It was rooted deep in the soul of a dancer that life must be reenacted through physical activity.

I am brokenhearted like a half-moon on its vanilla rim, forlorn in the despondent sky. Real blue, reminding the crestfallen field that we are not alone in this—although now downcast and mournful.

The call in ballet "to the barre," had interrupted her childhood reverie, and made graces out of clumsy adolescence. She would never forget the bright lights onstage, the music thundering into the auditorium. There was no first and last arabesque; it was if they had never danced before, and would never stop. Her hair had been slicked back with gel into a bun for most of her memories of dance, and her ballet slippers and leotard at practice were black.

We cannot know the sorrow life brings, nor count the mistakes we make, to give account; yet love has purchased us like slaves on the block, yoked us together and set us to work for a master we yet cannot see, without respite.

There was the expectant audience, waiting for a performance to summon them into applause. The ballerina would receive a bouquet of dozens of red velvet roses. It was daring to receive the honor, but even more daring to go home and be an ordinary person after the performance. The crowd would love the star. Again and again they would shout "encore".

If only we could be free from labor, and yet nature, every day, gives birth: the trees and roots expand, while flower opens, blooms, and dies. With this great power could we not harness the divine ones to come to our aid, wrest forgiveness, Ebony wrote.

She, too, would go home after this show, and have to be a normal person. The grace of the dance would follow her there. She would know her limitations because she was an athlete. There was no value in pretending to be needy. Why would she seek out other's pity by calling attention to her disease? It meant you were different than everyone else, and that would never do in the real world.

Chapter 18

Ebony hated the thought of becoming a marshmallow. She was deathly afraid of the marshmallow girl in the psych ward who was white as a dandelion that had gone to seed, with black hair and black eyes. Chloe's voice talked without an end to her sentences. Her words went on and on, trailed endlessly.

"Is this how people turned out on anti-psychotic drugs?" Ebony wondered.

When Ebony tried not to listen, Chloe spoke. She carried a Bible. Ebony felt helpless to change her. Was there anything that could be done for this overgrown rag doll with floppy limbs and a burned-out soul?

"Thorns tear the hand that touches them," Chloe said.

"That must be somewhere in the Bible," Ebony replied.

"All too true," she thought, "is that thorns are not usually rehabilitated with great success."

"Take your calcium and magnesium and you will not experience the tardive dyskinesia side effects of your medication," said her nurse while she tested her blood pressure.

The doctor further offered, "You may wish to have a visit with our psych ward nutritionist," he said. "I think she will be able to help you on the topic of how to prevent developing metabolic syndrome.

"It is important to stay well, both now and when you leave the hospital. Nutritious food is the building blocks of the body, and without it, health fails. The vibrancy and energy of a healthy person is what creates beauty and the enduring qualities we admire."

"There it was, plain as day—Beauty!" Ebony said nothing.

"Restoring the biochemical substances that promote health and wellness means eating right, supplements in appropriate quantities, exercise and rest. Learning to eat and cook with whole foods is a lifetime process that starts you on the road to success. Your nutritionist is teacher, educator, and lifetime learner of the nature and substance of food and nutrition," said the psychiatrist.

Every illness had a remedy. Ebony thought that the balm had always existed in nature somewhere. Her experience had led her to believe that every disease had a means of prevention and a way to healing. She observed the ways of the healers on earth and found their conclusions both profound and austere. She was not a doctor, but a scientist, following the forest, sighting nature, capturing a photographic imprint of her subtle impressions for naturalistic purposes.

The photographic painting was more than light and shadow. It was more than the brights of impressionism and imaginative color. It was more frugal than realism, with its dark slums and stark contrasts. The result soared over modern thought, as would the stillness of solitude over the roar of downtown traffic.

On the wall, it was almost fantastical: a woman in a purple dress who seemed of wealthy means entered a banquet hall with long white tables of tall white tapered wick candles, lit. There were ivory china plates and real silver, while the centerpiece was of evergreens. It hung in the psych ward hallway. Had they been summoned to a banquet, she wondered at the elegance.

Ebony looked out the window of her hospital room at the road with cars below. They passed by in all colors, the train of her postmodern thought—unlike a mosaic of stained glass windows at the Seminary of Christ the King, where she had taken the Mission Monastery exhibit. They held together in all their fragmented glory. Maybe her imaginary dreams were vanity; but they made her a good writer. One day she would pay the bills on her imagination, she thought. Her religion was the only thing holding her back. Somehow she knew she had to change it or it would change her.

She wrote:

The fine art of wicks, taught by yesteryear: beeswax, in the fine golden dark honey that melts in a puddle of riches here, tasted first when young and without money. Steeping tea to pour, peppermint gathers—tasted first without white cream or sugar. Seeing if we love herbs and hot water, speaking in a dialect of father. O beeswax, melting hotly in a crown, we take your candle to dark, gather round; seeing how we are justified by love and melting at the sight of heaven above. Bewitched by which is evil we succumb; and needing of the light we come undone.

Her thoughts of Catholicism, and the years of practicing religion rushed into her consciousness, "On the altar there are two beeswax candles—solemn towers, waiting to be lit, aflame—I, at the gate of the holy of holies, stand and wish my prayers to be heard: both in word and in deed, I pray, my hands blistered and bruised. I have prayed all night, and here I am, waiting.

"In the early morning, standing in a stream of colored light: red, orange, purple and aqua—the monks have all disappeared, the nave choirboys emptied the room long ago—only smoke, silence lingers. Feelings transmute into songs, moments become memories, facts become peals.

"Where information becomes reticent here— contemplations of revelation are austere minutes of our time on earth, therein dazzling us from mediocre to excel: the Madonna taking us by the hand with her son Jesus breathing the breath of our bones," she finished her prayer to Our Lady of Guadalupe.

"My spiritual practice should not have ended me here," Ebony thought. Perhaps being spiritual had cast her in a bad light, making her look feverish. She wondered what the best way would be to appear to the psych ward psychiatrist. This turn of events was making her rethink everything. Was she too stubborn to change?

Ebony woke suddenly. She had had a dream in which she was in heaven, bathing in an ivory pool, surrounded by lilies. There was a bulletin board and God would walk by and see what was new on earth. She could converse with him, but only because she was a spiritual being, and lived in a spiritual world.

The song of earth had spoken such meaningful words to me in the middle of the night, that I had become an Amazon River, with torrential rains in the jungle of my soul.

How was it that Ebony spent so much of her time in university composing melodies and lyrics while she yet studied Botany? Something drove writers to such extents; they were never happy without a pen in hand. Ebony compromised with her field journal, scrawling poems in between her observations.

Here is where the starlings tread the sky and find the air as they have always done. There was the canvas of the skies, and the feather brush, painting cloud and gold. Light is a beaded necklace of brown and indigo beads.

When she remembered her dream, she realized that in the spiritual world, she could post something on the bulletin board. It made a difference to her that someone upstairs was watching, that someone called the Divine would read it.

The starlings were without a brick and mortar home. They were without an altar or a shrine. Should we flit here and there as starlings with no recourse for our souls, save the conservatory of nature, the conservative country, the liberal landscape, melting heart hills, and opal moon?

When she heard what she had wanted to hear all her life, it was a song in the night. It was to her advantage that she wrote down each note. Black against the white page, they flew like starlings.

The blueberries in the fields disappeared like this thought or that thought, swallowed by the starlings—for they could not be guarded. They would wing free to another land that was starling country.

Ebony knew that once when she was out on the dikes, the trail on the outskirts of town, she had waded into the shallow irrigation channel on a sacred notion in her light-blue dress. She had bent beneath the waters as a form of baptism.

The starling dilemma: they lay in wait with cannons in the field, but there is a poignant uprising when the monastery tower rings over the valley. Religion was like diphtheria, to be inoculated against. Otherwise we stand as wise martyrs, had I the innocence of being the object that you loved...

She had emerged dripping and let her dress dry on the way home. What had she done it? There was no other way. She belonged to no one, or she belonged to the Divine completely.

The Queen of Starlings does look almost transient, but all birds return to the valley they own, dip over the flat olive fields. There is never even a doubt that if we had a difference of opinions, there'd be a parting of ways.

She had been a woman with a candle, writing once at City of Roses. Now the brokenness was a puzzle she put together each night by darkness, for she had nothing and no light.

All this in an uprising against the intellectual dictator, and the social barbs—the barbed wire fence.

"La chandelle est morte, je n'ai plus de feu," she thought. When the incense trailed heavenward, her emotions again translated themselves; write, she must, the very secrets of her soul or she would be a coward.

This is the limitless spirit world, where the cultivation of fields and the building of mansions evicts evil. There he is— standing in a tower of lapis lazuli; the light in his eyes has given him away.

Contemplations of Revelation

O true Ancient of Days,
O true mountain,
O true sure-footed deer,
O sign of eternal favor,
Run!

O only cave
Where four directions blow:
(North, East, South, West)
Listen!

O day of all earth's creation bright,
O night of constellations of the heavens,
Shine!

O Prayer for deeper meaning,
O Word for understanding,
O Diviner of the nature's song,
O Highlands of the earth's vast crags,
O Diversity of senses: vision, hearing, touch, taste,
Speak!

Part VI: The Philosopher

Chapter 19

A ruddy young man sat in the corridor and played his guitar. His eyes were deep and bright, and he had not lost his will to survive. He seemed there only over an accident. He wondered at the young woman's appearance in this place. Ebony showed him her book of photographs in black and white analog—a mossy barn, a field, the blackberry brambles, the free-wheeling sky. There was something there, behind the pictures that he could not quite place.

"Just think, you are like Joseph in the musical. How all the elements bow down to your camera, and you capture them, as a Joseph of old. You will soon rule the very ones who hated you, and they will bow before you begging for your mercy. They did not know you were planning an exhibit," he said with a smile.

"I am an abandoned child with no recourse. I cannot be permissive, or authoritarian to my enemies, for they have darkened my eyes in this place. I will only speak with authority," Ebony said. "I have many words to heal, and I bring order instead of chaos."

"Well done," said the young man.

He stared thoughtfully for a moment.

"What kind of patient is not allowed to choose healing over disease? And what remedy is ever forced upon the taker? What kind of woman is firmly barred from ever leaving lest she lose her sanity?" he asked of the silent corridor.

"You would escape, if given the chance," he said.

"*That one low call of evening, stuttered breath, arrested my thought and dragged it away: more than moving pearl sympathies in May, wildflowers for the heads of women, wreathed; children who would never tire and grow old playing forever in the dusty street—golden heads in a field of hard red wheat. Shivering by a heater in the cold, reciting civil lines of English verse. Hoping for the conscience's token piece, but subsisting on the fare of crabmeat, remnant of the blue ocean's salty purse. Whatever we may tire of while the poor, is now the indulgence of those with more,*" Ebony said, quoting a sonnet.

"Did you write that?" he asked.

Then the dream of freedom hurt her very soul, because it seemed an impossibility. Would she be forever a captive of a system she loathed? The young man was not ignoring her, and all of a sudden this moment in a lost place mattered. She would never forget her old ivy cottage by the lake, and liberty. Liberty would be the light in her eyes when she was finally free.

Ebony spoke very quietly, "*The dream is in my breast that rankled heart, dividing soul from mind, I tore the shame from my colorful dress, I wore the part—singing at first light, that his holy name were enough to make you steadfast, hungry for more of the spirit's tell movement. Light over the wild hills and valleys, lonely without a God that speaks in darkness, bright as the stars, sacrifice of silver youth."*

"Whoa," said the young man. "Speak up, let everyone hear you."

"I was sitting on the park bench, lithe. Watching the day go by as a sun-smooth dance: rehearsed, choreographed, classic tune. I am never more lovely than afraid," she said louder.

Ebony was a lily sheathed in white gown. The gossamer silk of a web woven as uniquely as the dew coated it with pristine gloss, and sunshine illuminated it, were the threads of her unique world. There was that reality of being a tree, and then the barrenness of its antiquity, the ancient path running beneath it, and the inquiring person now standing under its rustic leaves.

"Too old to live, too young to die." He looked up toward the light. What was once the sun became the moon. The earth was a watery canvas.

"The sun and skies abate their fury, mountain lions disappear into the wood in silent annulment of violence, the trees bend far over the water, until I bend and sway too—a dancer in the troupe of wind and cloud, a light ray of the noon, a figurative star alone on the horizon disappearing with the dawn," he said.

"You are a dancer in a Broadway musical over the silent type. Your world is brightly colored with emotion and words. I only thought to take a photograph, standing from afar, yet you enter into the fray of words—catapult their nonsense to and fro, rope them unlike animals in the circus, parade them around. And they are highly pleased," Ebony said.

They sat on the floor for awhile and traded reminiscences of freedom— those moments by the sea, or on the lake with the wind. They were two wilds meeting each other, shaking hands. When one wild soul meets another, they hardly start to think they should be more cultivated. They think they should be free.

"I'm caught in a moment, here with you," he said.

A woman was swearing loudly from the next room. The slavery of behavior modification had provoked her brave response of using the most powerful words she knew.

"Both the sacred and profane," Ebony answered, "are in the depth of the human soul."

"Ebony," he said. "What an interesting name."

"What is your name?" Ebony asked.

"My name is the philosopher," he said.

"Curious," she said. "I am a naturalist, and the ivy cottage is my home—right down the road from Hayward Lake."

"Shall we walk about?" he said.

"Sure. Where to?" she answered.

It was a beautiful sunny afternoon.

The philosopher said, "Why don't we walk around Mill Lake. We'll get a pass."

"Sure," Ebony said, hoping for an afternoon of freedom.

They were soon granted a pass, and walked around the lake path, conversing.

"What fine and decent young woman would not find adequate the shop of apparel and hats for an acceptable outing in the park? And respectable young men, suitors observe—the passable young lily, wreathed in pearl dew and her tolerable enshrouded morning," said the philosopher.

"The brilliance of siphoned immortality and glorious gesture, stooping in a vale—its majesty, righting all wrongs, fights, and sins, as flowers bloom and die, bold nobility their splendor, the chastening ode to the gods decked in every hue, and stateliness sublime," Ebony said.

"O curative sun and rain, list cloud above, your remedial persons fill earth—glory; yesterday, bracing the lungs with pure sweet air, and now reviving the constitution to move, bend, and breathe toward eternal patient love, vitalizing the lacking and deficient," said the philosopher.

They kept walking.

Ebony responded, "Far be it from me to pass into oblivion, when I could have made a difference. When we could have healed the ill with words that heal, instead of words that kill. I think they have heard too many hostile words, from both within and without."

"Words that kill, what an interesting theory," said the philosopher.

"Even a disease diagnosis could kill you if you expect you'll die," she said.

They walked along, observing the ducks and people passing. They came to the wooden foot-bridge.

"Sounds like a communication issue. People are too suggestible," he said.

"This is actually a scientific issue that could build a bridge between orthodox and natural medicine," she said.

"How so?" the philosopher asked.

"Because improving nutrition is the thing they both agree on. I think that communication affected by our nutrition is the missing link."

"How does nutrition affect our communication?" he asked.

"It has to do with cellular communication. Let me explain; the molecules of sugar that are attached in chains on each cell (polysaccharides) tell the cell what it does and what the other cells do. This allows them to communicate. When they can't communicate, it becomes the early onset of an auto-immune disease."

"What kind of sugar do we need for this to work," he asked.

"They are called essential sugars, and are usually bitter. If we don't consume these eight sugars every day, communication between cells eventually fails," she said.

"You know it's interesting that you say so, because I think, on another level, it could be a social thing as well. For example, this could be the cellular cause for miscommunication," he said.

"I'll agree with you," Ebony said, staring out over the lake as they crossed the bridge.

"Have you ever noticed other people around mental illness sufferers? People are not sure what they do for jobs, people think they might be dangerous, give wrong labels to them, and try to inject them with meds or have them put away? They can't identify their purpose, dreams, or goals in society."

"Okay, I've noticed that," she said. "I need a label stuck to my forehead that says I do work and therefore have purpose. Not only that, adults with mental illness are suspiciously regarded as childlike in their dependency."

"A social auto-immune disorder. Do we try to kill people that we think are the enemy. Do we try to punish them, when really they represent to us our lack of polysaccharides, the sugars on our cells that serve to identify others," he said.

"We don't even recognize people without some kind of label on their sweatshirt. We thought arthritis could be cured at the Gap. In the same way that we can't recognize cells without the sugar chain. They may be a foe or intruder, a mortal enemy, or a best friend," she said.

"Just think, tomorrow is a new day with no food trays in it yet," he said with a wink.

"Just drink the kool-aid," Ebony said.

"I thought you were going to say that the eight essential sugars are found only in healthy foods," said the philosopher.

"Okay, I'll tell you where they are found," she said.

"Soluble fiber—like oat bran and rice bran, sea vegetables, gums, beans, many fruits and vegetables, psyllium, glucosamine."

"You're right. I'll have to focus to eat those foods more," he said.

"We might think we have to get all the healthy nutrients to improve our physical bodies with some diseases; I think it's a daily war between life and death, in other cases, that is exemplified by our words to others. We are either winning or losing by what we say," she finished.

"Perhaps we shall do rounds of the psych patients when we return, and look them in the eye, and say to them: live!" the philosopher answered—"Yes, and we will say that our love is greater than all their experiences of hatred combined. They hate this place of barred doors, and sterile retribution. They hate that the only answer is mediation and precisely timed meals on beige trays, and then the psychiatric assays of their response. Yet they must be grateful."

"They guiltily drink the black coffee, because they sin if they hunger or thirst," Ebony said. "All their needs are accounted for here. Except love. For love is always a voluntary emotion and a choice of the indomitable human spirit."

Chapter 20

The naturalist and the philosopher returned to the hospital. As they walked down the squeaky hallway, their rubber soles rang out.

"Who would choose to love?" said the philosopher.

"Who can live without healing words?" Ebony responded as they walked to the nurses' station to sign in.

"Is not a child's greatest desire at birth to bond with their mother?" said the philosopher. "So it is in every action of gratefulness, we are bonding with the universe. We become children who are able to grasp the gifts held out to us. I think your gift is healing words," he said.

A week passed. Ebony had lived until this moment on the edge of a white hospital bed and waited for life to pass her by. All of life, so poignant and so cruel. It both loves and hates. It both kisses and curses. What of love or healing, except that which is forbidden, she thought.

The philosopher asked, "Shall we walk around the lake today?"

"Oh!" Ebony said, "How did you know about the trail around Hayward Lake?"

"Quite shortly, because it is forbidden," he answered. "The trail contains you, your shortcuts, and the long concentric paths of reasoning."

He said: "Beauty is forbidden love. Beauty reigns, Beauty rules over all. Take Beauty's cue and learn from the Queen of Ives, sitting at the great table of nature, pining o'er the crust of trees, icy streams, and censured lake haunt. She sees her reflection in the waters' mirror, bonds with solemn trust, always trysting for better light at nightfall."

Ebony said, "I cannot live without Beauty, for she is my right! I observe the ways of nature and compare them to humanity. I take note of the secrets of the wood, for it is my habitat and my home. "

Philosopher answered, "What a wild animal you are, hiding in the thicket. All of Beauty fades, and does so leave us. Noticing how the dawn becomes the scars of midday—bright as fawns, the planets circle nigh at dusk."

"I am a hideaway in the Canadian north, in the mountains of British Columbia. I have called the shores of this very lake my own. It is the perfection of life and livelihood I seek, and yet this is amoral. For how can I love anything so fleeting, so fanciful, and so destructive to womanhood as the shallows of what is perfection and then despair?" Ebony said.

Philosopher replied, "Beauty has no lasting life, forbidden as the secret tree; for she appears and disappears. What woman would aspire to this transience? She sings sweetly, but lasts but an hour. She falls like a petal to the ground, announcing her decay."

"Whisper to me in the wood of Beauty and her darkling speech," the naturalist said to the philosopher; for he thought the cold was cruel, and held her for warmth.

"No crackling fire exists in this neck of the woods, this sanctuary of stillness, this crown land of peaceful sacrifice to the wild," the naturalist said.

"We walk for quite some time, and hours pass before we eat our lunch of olive oil and bread, of almonds and peppers," said the philosopher.

"The dearest life of the trail is memory, that elusive force that beckons in the shadows of soul; for we will someday have no more recollection of the force that brought us here and called us to surrender, we will have only the memory of harmonics and the distance between us fading sharply," Ebony said.

"I will try to understand whether it was love or nature, that blew its quoted tune, the nightingale sounding a sweeter trill, rippling over trees, and leaves, and lakeside," said the philosopher.

The deep call of a singing bird from the blackberry thicket interrupted their reverie.

Ebony spoke to the philosopher, and said: "I will not be turned back, for now I and Beauty are one. She is my mountain mirror; the stream is my drink; the field, my food. The animals draw near to observe my gentle ways."

"Beauty is falsehood, and must be more fleeting than ugliness. From what school of thought do you dissolve all that is imperfect, and absolve those righteous with perfect face and figures. Death comes early to those who work their way to Beauty, for it is the path to the grave," he said.

The philosopher and the naturalist talked for awhile in the hospital cafeteria. There were dreams, then there was the modern world, then there was reality. They seemed to be here in a pleasant space, not succumbing to mental disorder in the orderly precise routine of the hospital day. Yet they could succumb to dreams of who they were, gardens of dreams beyond these hallways and locked doors.

The philosopher took her to her home when he could: the wild wood of her lake shore. There they sat in the living room of the ivy cottage. The Wanderer sat before the hearth one evening; he pulled from his pack a wooden flute and it gave a sonorous tune.

"I will return to where the river meets the sea," he sang, "I call the vast place of waters my home. For I was conceived in the primordial ocean—within the saline waters of her wave, covered by the deepest blue—Washed over until I was sculpted like fine marble into a human form. There, my spirit moved and my body became the philosopher."

"When I invite you, it is communion that embraces you; the community of koinonia recreates humanity into orderly love, repairing all that is damaged, cleaning all that is soiled, feeding all those who hunger, speaking life to the poor, serving the weak," Ebony said.

She continued, "I was birthed in a fiery inferno in time, descended from a star. I was haloed in its cosmic center and ransomed from its regal heart. My creation was a myth borne on the wings of a pegasus. My birth was legend and I am folklore of the gods. I am righteous as my mentor, stolen as the ripest nectar."

The Wanderer considered deeply, for he was the philosopher, and she the naturalist—memorizing each bird and stone, so the queen's song of nature allured his senses and he said, "Let me sleep here until morning."

Her heart was hidden in the depth of the night, her spirit darkened, and the philosopher consented to light her candle. His request was to sit here at her feet, and eat of her table, for it was plentiful.

Ebony awoke at an early hour, and began to prepare for the day. Ebony prayed for her soul and its preparation for the Divine. She prayed for those who were children after her ways. She prayed for the earth, that it would not fall into corruption and dissolve.

The light in the sky was moving quickly toward morning. The birds began their song, woven into the quiet of the lake, where peace was its mantle. So the naturalist and the philosopher decided to walk each day on the path around the lake, to roam and swim together, yet free in their daily journeying through the forest, until they one day reached the other side.

 **Chapter 21**

"Ebony," a voice sounded over the hospital loudspeaker. "You can see the nutritionist now."

Ebony entered the nutrition office hesitantly. She was immediately put at ease by the big chairs and petite woman with glasses behind the desk. The nutritionist took out a clipboard and had her fill out some data. Then she asked how Ebony`s meals were going, and what she like to eat usually at home.

"I may be somewhat different that the hospital dietician," she said, looking Ebony in the eye. "I am a food counselor who helps people process their issues around eating and diet. I am interested in your life and what you know."

"Sure. That sounds interesting," Ebony said.

"I have learned from your chart that you had an eating disorder once. Did you suffer from anorexia?" she asked.

"Yes, I did," Ebony replied. Suddenly she longed to talk to this woman about what hurt and what healed people like her.

"I was seventy-eight pounds when I was twenty-one years old," she said.

Ebony thought again about the wild horse of hunger. It occurred to her that many times she had gone without adequate nutrition, and it seemingly no longer mattered to her. But the wild horse knew. He had been tamed once. He had cantered in a corral of the mind, and been harnessed up under the powers of a nutrient-rich lifestyle.

Ebony said, slowly, "I was dependent on the hand that fed me, and the motive behind it. But if in the beginning I was reaching out for food in acceptance, I would one day know that if the hand stopped feeding me or disappeared, I would disappear also. I would adopt a skeletal frame and emaciated form, with bony protrusions. I would dream of food only, and reject it in person. I would claim to have already eaten, and then cut up miniscule morsels of cantaloupe as my day's wages," she continued.

She replied, "It is my purpose, my life's calling to see in everyone that possibility for good nutrition, and unbroken health. This is my philosophy; for if there was no hunger, there would be no eating disorder. At some point when we have moved beyond hunger to invincibility, to not needing, we may become the mother or father ourselves, the adored one. All food stems from this source, from first milk, and we know that bonding is the reassurance that a relationship forms to continue interdependence.

"When we look into the eyes of our guardian, we are secure that their love will be evident in the feeding of their offspring. We know the danger of ever being separate from this source, and the insecurity of pain or fear," she continued.

"There is a discomfort when a baby cries, for there is a need that their hunger or thirst be filled. I know that beyond that there is reassurance that the need will always be filled, that the child will never go hungry or be unable to access the resource of food appropriately—because relationship will always exist, as long as there are people on this planet," she said.

"I can see you have thought about this a great deal, and probably gone through much therapy already," the nutritionist said. "To encourage you, no longer must a patient dwell for years on end with no cure in sight and no means for recovery. Food that is energetically sound is the healer, and will nourish every cell as appropriately deserved, now, with your permission."

"I agree," Ebony said.

"Then let's try this exercise. I will ask you to affirm again now, as on the day of your birth, when you were born into this world. Food is essential for life, and you affirm its goodness and nourishment to you each time you eat. You are assured again and again of its power both to hurt and to heal you. You are now the bearer of a gift of knowledge that will take you beyond this place of fear and disease to wholeness and healing. Feeding the planet and the children of tomorrow is begun one person at a time."

Ebony repeated her words.

"What draws us away from hunger as a vice," the nutritionist continued, "resting our emotions from need and the burdens of want, is the returning again and again to our source. Society runs like clockwork, never failing, never tiring, predictable as it is unpredictable, and constant as mother and father at providing resources."

"Yes," said Ebony.

"The higher quality of food you choose, the greater will be your success—as the value is in choosing food that heals," said the nutritionist.

When the nutritionist's door closed behind her that afternoon, Ebony knew something different about the world, hunger, and herself. What she had desired to verbalize for so long had suddenly been put into words by someone who thought about needs and wants as deeply as herself.

She had been a deadly anorexic once. The sweat had trickled as she ran the miles in rehearsal for the race and the medallion. She ran day after day, to win. She would be the runner who was undaunted at life's task and death's mystery. She would take the challenge, and be a victorious athlete. She was willing to subdue her body, and ignore the burning of her muscles, desirous for the cries of vicious exhaustion to end, and find the final exhilaration of the ribbon. She had run in the snow, in the dead of winter, and she felt it now. Ebony's mantra hung over the heads of her doctors and therapists: clear, clear as the basin of green called Hayward that reflected her soul. It was *"Be"*.

The day was rainy and grey from the windows of the hospital. Ebony looked for a notice on the psych ward bulletin board to indicate how soon she could expect to leave and go home. There was only a phone number for scheduling a review panel hearing. She wrote down the phone number.

Ebony turned around. She looked like a child in the sterile hallway. She was wearing the blue hospital slippers. The philosopher was strumming his guitar.

"In every endeavor, let there be peal of every heartbeat's thunder loud, creed from minds of persuasion's honor cloud, harbinger of happenstance destiny," he sang.

"The moment I enter the room, you catch my eye and welcome me—for I am a vessel steeped in fine perfume and oil," the naturalist said.

"I can follow your essential oils all the way down the hallway," said the philosopher. "You must believe in their therapeutic value or you would not use them in such quantity."

"That is only too true," she sighed, "I bought two hundred dollars worth of eucalyptus and clove oil this year. One is heating and one is cooling."

"Heating and cooling, heating and cooling. Sounds like the hydrotherapy they have to endure at old psychiatric institutions like Riverview," said the philosopher. "You are both fiery and chilling."

"Riverview," Chloe said, as she walked by, "the very name puts cold fear into the heart of any psych patient. The final threat towards their incompliance is that they be shipped off to the old graveyard for good."

"Chloe, how could you," Ebony responded.

"I'm only telling you what will happen if you don't."

"Saltiness of a thousand beads of sweat, running down the face of the toiling; to those I cry, 'Freedom!'" said the philosopher.

"Freedom, you may pay the price," the naturalist said.

"In the old days people in those asylums could die of mania," the philosopher said.

"I have asked all my life for Beauty's graces, her tempered horse of virtue, her silver piccolo tapering the high notes. In my youth, it refused me to eat, hoping I would become thin and stay meager. As an adult, I would reject such thoughts as vanity or fear, and seek perfection in art. Is not art immortal, and stays itself on earth when all else is lost?" Ebony asked.

"Immortality!" he thundered. "How so does one seek immortality, or use it as a vice. This difference of caste between you and all those that are poor—will your photography ever be priced below the millions—for you are a noblewoman.

A writer believes words never fade. That is only because men commit themselves to the memorization of verse, while paintings age, and photographs fade in light. Destroy the negative, and the price of a photograph may go up fifteen-fold."

"My father once told me—examines your motives for success, and the success of others. Perhaps you will find society in general rewards those who seek the high road. Yet the high road is this: teach your soul to be humble and put others first, you will only benefit, regardless of your intelligence," she said.

"If we can harness a Jungian philosophy of symbolism together, our capability and resourcefulness, you can travail once again to reach your goals and find satisfaction that you have done your life justice. For each life is valuable in its contribution to the whole, and thus life has innate value, not only in what it is, and how it appears, but in what it can be transformed into," he said.

Contemplations of Revelation

O true Son,
O true beat of blood in my veins,
O true bow and arrow,
O hunter of the dream world,
Find wisdom's day and night!

O only accepter
of the way things are and the way they are not,
(accept, bear, fight)
Grow courage!

O strength of my now aging bones,
O character of the courageous home,
Return to your source!

O Child of the cooking fire,
O Youth of forest's hierarchy,
O Man of hunt and gathering,
O Leader of a tribe,
O Way through the wilderness,
Set out upon the journey!

Section VII: The Castle

 **Chapter 22**

"Eternal life means something of you will never die," Ebony said. "Do you know we're spirit beings?"

"You know I believe in an after-life," said the philosopher.

"Okay, but what does it look like?" asked Ebony.

"I think I should describe to you the Prince of Alchemy, for he is a person of myth and parable," said the philosopher.

"To tell you the story, I would have to begin at the very place of a garden," he said.

"Our Lady as she was called, lived in the Castle of the Moon. The castle spires and towers rose into the mist on the hill where she dwelt on an island by the sea. The city in which she lived bloomed all year around with roses and daffodils. The trees flowered in white, and their delicate lace of blossoms covered the ground, over which the docile horses pulled carriages year in and year out.

"Our Lady was as beautiful as the night in full bloom, with long dark hair and wide brown eyes. She wore a medieval gown with beaded bodice, and had the emblems

of four empires embroidered on her skirt, symbolizing the
symbols in ironwork on the common's door.

"The people of the city did not notice Our Lady and
her job that kept her busy most of the time behind the
curtain. She sat at the window in the tower from which
she would look out on the countryside. She bent her head
over her writing desk, and, with quill and ink, wrote
down the prayers of the people. She sat there most of the
day, and this kept her busy when she was not tending the
flowers in the garden, or burning incense in a golden
bowl.

"She was a skilled gardener, and so her flowers grew in
beautiful array and her closest friend was the unicorn. He
was a gentle prophet who understood great visions and
contemplated with much understanding.

"'For we live in heaven, and they live on earth,' said
the unicorn.

"The silence grew, every blade of grass, every tree bore
the fingerprint of time: 'Go deeper, deeper,' the Queen of
Ives called.

"The unicorn bowed his head. 'At the beginning, the
world was young. Its fruitfulness fed the earth—now it
has grown old, and the earth goes hungry. Where will we
find the harvest to feed our young before they die?'

"Then silence.

"The unicorn said, 'I will prophesy of the unknown
and the unseen; I will sing a song in the morning and tell
a tale in the evening. With every star in its place, I dictate

order from chaos, and measure out the ways of both animals and people like a recipe.

"'I will take my place at the table beside the Queen of Ives, Mother Nature. I will learn of her winds and seasons, her rains and snows, her hurricanes and thunderstorms. Her children brought from the four corners of the earth speak in the language of both earth and heaven, they know the time measured out for them to prophesy. They speak and the world does not understand them, in riddles and dark speech.'

"The table was set with fine food and red wine, followed by dessert: chocolate snowflakes; everyone ate his fill. Then Our Lady rose and addressed those invited: 'Forget not the statutes of the deep, the riddle of love and commitment, the fire of the hearth which glows bright in the eyes of those who have made heaven their home.'

"Our Lady said, 'The Queen of Ives takes each meadow by the hand as a young child, and adorns it with the flowers of solitude. She gives each swallow a home. Her earthquakes shake the foundations of the world, her precepts clothe the rolling hills and plains, the mountains resonate with dawn's first light. In all seasons, she rules the night with constellations.

"'The animals and people of the earth are subject to her mercy. She rewards those who diligently plow the land, those who replant the deserts of Israel with citrus and myrtle.

"'A people made their way through the desert once, and now they are scattered over the whole earth. Yet everyone has their needs and desires, their deep hunger for the Divine; and the people I chose are now my own. Like an ornate tapestry hanging on the wall of the banquet hall where we make our choice of nourishment each day, is this people.

"'Decked in tradition and holy law, Israel carries the message of long-awaited hope. Its flavors steep like fine tea, and its bread without leaven bakes for century after century in remembrance of the word of the Divine, and in deep commitment to his community.'

"The unicorn spoke, 'One day his people will again find their home in the land that was given to them. The redeemed will return to the Divine, and the city of the king. They will dance in the streets of the heavenly realms, and the laughter of women and children will once more symbolize peace. Every man will know that the pain of suffering is gold, and the truth of the old stories will again resound like the beating of a heart.

"'The glory of the Divine shines through the deepest sorrow, admonishing it to submit to his presence and power both in the present and in the future to come. When Israel becomes ready, she will arise as a bride and decorate herself, awaiting her bridegroom.

"'Oh sweet spires, reaching to heaven in the middle of the night. Your cathedral echoed a mighty chorale, a precise fugue, its stained glass of saintly icons memorized the nature of perfection in those who follow the child and his nativity.

"'The stones of your establishment know the truth of holiness when they inspire your servants to love others more than themselves, to lead as shepherds with a following of sheep.

"'The Divine has called you and set you apart for the things of spirit above flesh. You must rise above the vices of your counterparts, you must reason with the Divine, you must go on when you fail, and sing even though you may be in mourning. Gloria.

"'When night falls, lift up your voice like a watchman on the walls, call out over the ramparts that all is well to your people, warn them in danger, admonish them to love peace and to fight for what they love.

"'Your love must be tempered by commitment, your beauty tempered by kindness, your peace tempered by strength. Then your heart must resound with the things above. In all, you will find what you search for most when you lay down what you have prized above all else, when your secret treasure becomes your eternal home in the place where you will live forever.

"'Time is but the passing of notions, the blink of an eye, and all must rest on the foundation that was created before the world began of unity, belonging, and the need for family. The deepest possession of a man on earth is his love for his wife, and her jewel is her brood of children,' said the unicorn."

The philosopher continued his story:

"Our Lady replied to the unicorn, 'Now you will eat at our table and drink the noblest of wines, but tomorrow you must go into the Palace of Alchemy and sit beside the prince. Offer him your myth and your name Rhema, and he will be grateful to you. Tell him of the old ways, and the precepts that are not of men but of angels. Let the language of verse be your medium, and he will be delighted that you are full of riddles.'

"Our Lady's long dress was aqua, and she wore a circlet of gold with diadem; her words were always very eloquent, and her manners equally amiable. Those who sighted her on earth were said to be prophets of sainted vision. So the unicorn went into the temple. There was a circle of prophets on the mosaic floor. They surrounded the white unicorn and bade him enter the realms of earth. Their call was heard, so he disappeared and reappeared at once in a beautiful garden.

"There were a good many flowers and shrubs, all carefully pruned, of English varieties, paper-thin in every color. It was the garden of the Palace of Alchemy. A young man was sitting by the window and looked out over his prized flowers—there he saw the unicorn, drinking from the fountain.

"'What manner of species is that?' he questioned, and rushed out to find a unicorn in his garden, drinking peaceably.

"The young man was delighted to find such a beautiful creature as the unicorn, and walked about the paths with him for quite awhile.

"'I am of the myth, and my name is Rhema,' said the unicorn. 'I come from the heavenly realms, and have appeared on earth for a certain time, to minister to your Lord,' he said to the young man with golden hair whom he knew was the Prince of Alchemy.

"The prince agreed that he had never before seen such a creature, though he had a livery of horses, thoroughbreds and stallions. He had visited many countries on earth, and had not come across any mythological beasts in them. Not even in India, where he had visited the Taj Mahal had he seen such a great talking beast," said the philosopher.

Chapter 23

"The prince was very educated in science, math, art, and astronomy. This unicorn must have indeed come from heaven, he thought. He listened closely to Rhema's words, which rang like bells over the lawns, and walked with him in the garden for many days.

"'You are an alchemist and listener,' Rhema said.

"The unicorn told him that the people of the end times had a need for his alchemy, for they were being transformed by suffering from base metals into gold. Their martyrdom was their greatest gift to Our Lady.

"The prince ascertained that it was indeed what one gives to others that make one wealthy in heaven and not on earth. For to seek gain would undermine the heavenly kingdom, at whose gates many were now waiting to enter.

"'But there must be another who will go before them and create a way through her own martyrdom. There must be a way into the heavenly realms through the ebony and the ivory gate,' said the Prince.

"'The Prince of Alchemy will marry his bride,' Rhema said. And her name will be Israel. She wanders on the hillside like a young shepherdess. The elements bow to his majesty, for he has taken the base and dross of this earth to create the treasure of the divine. He transmutes iron and copper into gold and silver through suffering.'

"'Take heed of his counsel, ask of him his cup of suffering to be poured out on this earth, that we might be changed before the great day of the elect by the martyrdom he has chosen for his people.

"'Israel is the chosen of earth and her horn is of plenty: what a lovely dress of the nations she wears, for her people cover the earth like the sand of the seashore. Her hair is glossy, like the mane of a horse and her skin is anointed with fine perfume. She will return from the desert and hear the words of the prince, speaking to her heart, asking for her hand. Let us be resonant martyrs of this deeper love, agape, that would ask us come and give all to enter the eternal realms and witness this bride of his youth.'"

The philosopher said, "Listen to the sound of the wind in the trees. Listen to the stars converse. Listen as the planets converge. Listen to the night. Listen to the Milky Way. Listen to the day. Listen to the wind and sun. Listen to the desert flower. Listen to the child at play. Listen to his mother.

"The Prince of Alchemy has made them all—diverse and colorful as the nations, he holds creation in his hands to extract the finest ore, shine the dross gold. Listen to the naturalist, and you will hear him speaking to his bride."

"The Prince of Alchemy said to the bride: 'In Israel, miles away, awash under an olive grove, I took your hand once and showed you my castle from afar. High up on the hillside overlooking the valley, light beckoned from every window, and the halls, ornate and unchallenged, rhymed with insight.

"'Now, as a young woman, you stand on the brink of eternity, and the kingdom of the earth is shrouded—in an opaque layer of tales, myths and legends, rivals to the throne, or illustrious co-patriots of it.

"'Fantasy is the buffer between sanity and reality. The chasm of indivisible hearts divided by terror is seldom crossed except in the imaginary world. O Israel, the bride, I led you into the darkness once of the reality world and showed you the unimaginable terror.

"'Israel, I stood in the night and called for your song. I still ask for your heart, and your favor.'"

"Israel said, 'My tears fall as I remember the days of my youth—the destruction of my temple and my people. My sacred Scriptures remain to this day, and you can ascertain what their meaning is.'

"'For even Our Lady in the heavenly realms has not forgotten me in this time of the end,' said Israel. She will send a unicorn to aid you, named Rhema. The white unicorn will come to you in the Garden of Alchemy, and will reveal the truth of the oracle to you, the message that was sent and the last prophecy.'

"The Prince of Alchemy replied, 'I will wait until this messenger is sent to me, for my love is greatest at the time of the end toward my people, I understand their suffering and its reason: I will yet see them chaliced gold when Israel returns to the place of her first love, and becomes my bride.'

"'I see a thorn of crowns. In the night, the stars are my burning eyes roaming to and fro. I seek over the whole earth for those constant in trial, and persevering.'"

"On coronation day, the prince entered the coronation hall. The colorful flags of the nations were flying over the sea. His procession halted at the Iron Gate. He turned, bade farewell to his princely days and faced forward to assume his new role as king. The crowd jostled for position, cheering and waving. The king would take the throne.

"The unicorn Rhema stood by his side as he took the scepter and wore the jeweled crown, emerald and ruby with inlaid diadem; he waved to the people of his heart.

"With a constitution of praise the prince would have a long and fruitful reign, for he benefitted all those he touched. Many came from miles around to hear his wisdom, and the sick lifted their heads when he touched them saying, "The King touches and God heals."

"The nation's coin bore his image so that he could bestow on each person he touched the blessing of the touch piece. The copper coin was inscribed with the words: Sol Deo Gloria.

The unicorn Rhema bowed his head. His time on earth seemed drawing to a close. He could feel the court of the prophets pulling him heavenward once again to Our Lady. The distinctive sound of a bell could be heard, ringing its descant, sonorous—calling:

"'Return, O unicorn, for the time of the last prophecy is soon over.'

"The last prophecy! The unicorn felt his chest swell with importance, but he knew one must wear humility to enter again through the Ivory Gate. He bowed his head and disappeared.

"The unicorn entered through the Ebony Gate, praying the first prayer:

"'My steady constitution has been fortified by loving-kindness, by the practice of rising early, and dissolving in prayer my sins, and the sins of others. I enter by the ebony gate, as do all who are sinners. I call upon the patience and goodness of Our Lady to benefit my spirit. I bear the blood of my fathers, the guilt of my mothers, and I am overcome by dread at my dream of paradise. Yet this is my one request.'

"The unicorn entered through the Ivory Gate, praying the second prayer:

"'I am lonesome and nothing without you, my constant companion and friend: the one who adores me without hesitation. You are my dominant force, and fluent in prayer over me. I pray to come into your kingdom at a young age and follow your ways. All who ask of me, hear of your goodness. I enter by the ivory gate, as do all who are children, and know no evil, modest and chaste, singing the hymn.'

"The unicorn entered the third gate, the Way I Pass Through, praying the third prayer:

"'I pass through when on my knees in prayer. I commit myself to the eternal Divine, decide that mercy is enough, and contemplate holy perfection that outweighs all my attempts to become beautiful. For mercy is the face of Our Lady. And so I come, with every breath I breathe, here silenced by your face, you took my shame, your love became my peace, and all my sorrows bore.'

"The unicorn entered the fourth gate, Prayer for my Countrymen, praying the fourth prayer:

"'I pray for all my countrymen who have refused to stay silent anymore—may they stand tall on behalf of their country, for dark times have come to many on earth. They might weep if they were not proud, and might bow to evil if they could not resist. So stand, the resistance, for you are not victims anymore, but harbingers of the last prophecy. Once my sweat trickled in the dust like liquid silver, and it was enough to embrace poverty and hard work—but now, we are after the treasure we seek.'

"The unicorn entered the fifth gate, Prayer for my Aging Body, praying the fifth prayer:

"'The light to bear at my humble last breath, the goblet of oil, cast out purest gold, all speak of favor's now placed laurel wreath—the best reward when I am creased and old. I shall with folded hands, resting, here pray for my heart's desire to not be lost when I am gone, and the print words to not stop saying all that was delicate and austere then.'"

The unicorn was now in the fifth heaven. This is where creatures such as himself lived in harmony with other spirit beings. The seventh heaven was reserved for those who composed melody, lyric, and verse. The seventh heaven was where the first strains of a symphony resounded. From the clarinet to the French horn, this was where those who knew musicianship dedicated their spare moments, for no time is wasted under the skill of a master. The master of them all, who had uttered the first note, was still singing.

Contemplations of Revelation

O true Elder,
O true watcher of the people,
O true gain of wisdom,
O spirit of times past,
Remember!

O only illuminator
of the three dimensions of time,
(child, parent, elder)
Re-light!

O smoldering smudging burning,
O lighted flame of future vision,
Reignite!

O Sound advice from depth of night,
O Spirit of the ancient's word,
O Dreamer of the life beyond,
O Wind of legend north,
O Teacher of the ways of earth,
Redirect!

Section VIII: The Lens of Pathos

Chapter 24

"The Queen of Ives is the one we reckon with for our very lives," the philosopher thought out loud, "for she is mother of us all. Both creator and destroyer, the powerful force behind the gales, the monsoons, she ices the north, and rears up in the Midwest."

"My lens captures the lake—flora and fauna, woods and bird's nests in black and white. I carry my camera on the forest trail, I make the bearded wood my subject and it worships me; but then, I will never find another as beautiful, who reigns, Mother Nature, over us all," the naturalist said.

"The Queen of Ives—black diamonds in her hair, sapphires at her throat, rubies course in her veins, her look is one of trust amid adversity," the philosopher replied.

"And what adversity," she moaned, "for the most terrible of worlds has come upon us. We are trusting of people who have certified us on dogma. There is no law to protect us, and they claim it is in the name of charity. What recourse do we have to even walk out our lives of peaceful non-violence; to live in harmony with nature? We are prisoners, in no unequal terms, mere chattels."

"Will you fly the great eagle's soaring wingspan,   .
elucidate the clouds' passing dreams, enter the vast arena
of nature, witness of her streams, lashing winds oft her
arms. Screaming for a better place in the dark depth of
wood where no one ever hears, etching the surface of
night," said the philosopher.

"I cannot be any animal but the eagle, for they live on
the heights. Their soaring wingspan has lifted me far
above my counterparts. I enter the eye of the storm. I
resound in the heavens. Surely I will find my final home
when the storm has abated," the naturalist said.

A nurse passed by with the lunch trays. The metal cart
rattled in the hallway. The naturalist and the philosopher
began to walk toward the lunchroom, unmoved by the
schedule of mealtimes and aroma of hot soup. They sat in
the lunchroom. Ebony thought, "Bearded Wanderer in
this place, with brown eyes and bright vision—walk the
walk benign around the pathway, blaze the trail unfound
in your eyes until you behold Mother Nature, pristine,
untouched and virgin-young. She sings and the signs
appear."

She wrote in her field journal:

One by one we would read them, showing the way before us,
one testimony, we would heed them, treading down the ancient
railway's path. Yet I remain here, ever-true; my heart raptures
wherever I walk in these streams, carved out one day by my
lonesome hike, made for two creatures who loved.

.204.

We might have tired on the journey if we were not two lovers hand in hand: loving an old Railway Trail, loving the Divine's triune light.

What mystery unravels like the trail? We follow the footsteps of days gone by, we whisper in the silence then laugh out loud. Of time and the forest, the forbidden love that years do not dissipate is suddenly consummate.

Where the orange sun spears the silent sky, traverses across the day, disappears with the night we vow to never leave our intimacy.

Later, the philosopher sat in the corridor with his guitar. He sang quietly, "Way Beyond the Blue."

"I've got a home in glory land, you can come too..."

"Way beyond the blue," Ebony joined in.

"I would like to go for a walk around outside the hospital," he said.

They both obtained permission from the nursing station, and exited the hospital to walk outside. It was almost winter. The leaves were a dull burgundy, turning and littering the sidewalk with color. The wind was chilling.

Ebony put on her black gloves. She had twenty pairs of black gloves at home. Here she had only one. Mrs. Velvet had always said she had piano fingers, but without gloves she was cold.

They walked by the large round cement planters. Ebony had helped the occupational therapist plant flowers that past summer. When they weren't planting flowers, they worked on projects daily in the occupational therapy room, such as painting ceramics, leatherwork, or making bath salts. Every day they played a different game together to increase their skills. She was knitting a green and white cotton scarf.

The philosopher stopped suddenly, staring intently into Ebony's gold-rimmed eyes.

"This has occurred to me," he said, "and I have been thinking it over. The Queen of Ives reigns supreme in the heavens, making way only for the Prince of Alchemy—turning base metals into gold from a long time ago. His subjects are devoted to his every cause, and sit in the night as darkened spires waiting for morning."

"Watchmen, who wait in the night, hope for the morning, it will illumine all that is shrouded for death and clothe it with day's light," Ebony said.

"The Queen of Ives is mother of us all," continued the philosopher. "She doubled over in fiery pain to release us and each star appeared, burning its way through the galaxy. She swallowed the goldenrod, and birthed each sun and moon. She grew a garden of vegetables with food for every season, grew from her tree olives and apricots, and from her soil garlic and onions."

The naturalist replied, "Deep within the deepest wood she hides, as modest as a young woman with a velvet hood, she sings to all who dare hear:

"My sister, the fields
My brother, the mountains
My mother, the moon
My father, the sun
My wild fare feeds you
My neck of night embraces you
with stars, a diamond necklace
My eyes are made of rock planets that turn to and fro."

"The Queen of Ives is both creator and destroyer of all nature," he said, "bringing it up from the earth, and then swallowing it beneath the salty waves. The mighty Queen of Ives—the earth is her cathedral, her vast consecrated temple, she hovers over the altar, and calls to lovers, 'Come inside and be married,' coaxing them to unite as family and have children. She is the realm of the fertile in the heart of love: the stained glass of sunset's last glow, the spiritual fervor of a burning fire. She is the priesthood, presiding over the harvest, and the ocean's motherhood, salty waves of blessing."

"Rivet me and my eternal soul," the naturalist said, "for I know the Queen of Ives would dare me to outlive my fellow man. Yet she could not commit treason against the infinite Prince of Alchemy. For she is both nature and immortal—standing, and fallen as the snow. She is poured out like rain, and shouts like thunder."

"'Brethren,' she calls, standing in a river of fear and shame, deep as the Ganges, 'leave your mother and your brothers and follow the blue moon home to where the nightingale hides,'" said the philosopher.

The naturalist and the philosopher had not yet realized that in their minds, they could be free.

Chapter 25

The naturalist and the philosopher sat in the cabana looking out over the lake before dawn. The philosopher was strumming his guitar. His chestnut hair fell over his eyes. He sang, and she listened on the inside, while on the outside she calmly ate her breakfast of corn flakes and soy milk in the hospital lunchroom. The things they shared meant he was a person she could not do without. His person was extending to her a kind invitation, he was not seducing her. Yet madness was seductive, the psychiatrist had said. She must not let psychosis take over her mind.

"The puritan last hour, strong and docile inviting ovation from wind and night. Mention of her meditation, the still heart of a novice steeled for dark and light and the lonesome task of kind poverty. The kaleidoscope of beauty's chaste might makes order out of gray misery."

Ebony went back to her room. She wrestled inside with the fear that comes after anxiety; a chilling cold that crept through the floors of the hospital and into her fingers. They were the same fingers that had once deftly hammered out notes on the piano and practiced scales. Then it crept into her feet, the same feet that had once put on her ballet slippers, and spun in dazzling pirouettes.

She opened her eyes. She could hear the philosopher talking in the hallway and realized she had been dreaming.

"At the junction of silver time and space the invisible touching nocturnal—all that sweats beneath the hardship of place, where, gathered to work under eternal planets collected, a starry bouquet; mentor, fatherly and loud, visible to endorse the healing pale tourniquet," his voice boomed.

Ebony was not sure what the answer was to this complex mathematical equation. She did not have the skills to answer. She had to get away from the hospital, but she was not sure how. The complex web of her life had become so entangled that she was helpless. The only people who had visiting rights in this cold, white, and sterile place had committed her.

"Powers faintly endeavor, nor succumb delineate each custom note in time—purchase the tempo of the yellow sun, measure the meter of the moon's white shine. Speak, Champion, an orator of peace. Congress bares its cheek: unlikely chaperon with burden to admonish hatred cease," the philosopher announced, looking in at her.

The naturalist wrote in her field journal:

When the cattails in the wetlands turn rust, and the light draws shadows over the pond, I sit in my cabana as I must, and in all time's ways, chance to look beyond. I can feel the silence, blue-

steady, here and each dark night is but the canvas for a shooting star.

Each heaven bares its soul at red dusk's rest, showing off its shoulder beneath the white neck of space, black as a star-strung velvet dress, the first spance of light, untimed yet correct in every vision, drifting dream of day now shouting down its fury of the way the ill and old are left forgotten too.

Who is uncared for in this land of bloom, are not the gardens weeded, reaped? What careless oversight leaves some to gloom, and children, not their benefactors meet? Do mothers sweep a dusty hovel, old with cares before the bright-winged 'morrow told of its centered universal night-light.

The philosopher looked over the still wide surface of Hayward Lake. "We bow our heads each morning. We stop and contemplate. We pray simply, inviting Wisdom to lead. As we ready our minds to listen we are partakers in a divine legacy of listeners: we hear the voice of direction and leadership of the spirit of the Divine. This place in the womb of God is holy and pure, protected."

Ebony began to feel panic that her psychiatrist did not really understand her, that she should tell someone the truth about her mind; that she was really normal. This wasn't what it seemed. Her mouth went dry.

"We are here in the womb, until we are born into an eternal heaven at the end of our days—we are created and formed until we are full-grown and ready for birth into the heavenly realms," the philosopher prayed.

"For we are not uncultivated and overgrown," the naturalist said out loud, "but gardens sewn with order and care, weeded and pruned, tended by a gardener who knows each flower: we are desired—sought after, plucked, as a red rose in bloom, cherished in each dimension of our soul, creatures of many facets."

"We know the order of a Creator that usurps chaos," said the philosopher, "the truth that supersedes deception, the love that overcomes all evil, and will pass through the ebony and the ivory gate."

Ebony knew that there was something she would be given in return for what she had gone through. She knew that keeping up appearances all these years for the other people in her life had eroded the fabric of her personhood. She had thought that perhaps quietly resting here would help it be restored, but no one listened to her. She was only given medication against her will. She wrote a note for the psychiatrist. The nurse took it at the nursing station and tucked it into her book.

"What will you give as a gift in return for all that has been given you? What will you offer for love where intimacy with the divine has now claimed you and named you—captivated, enthralled—has purchased your soul, and said "you belong." Does this critical idea now hold weight in a place deeper than hate?" asked the philosopher.

Ebony swallowed hard. "I do believe in you," she said to the Divine. "I will admit it, I need you now."

"For you were called abandoned. You were called forgotten. No one to plead your cause. No one to bring you back from the desert. But the Divine hath loved you," the philosopher said.

Ebony wondered if the Divine really could help her.

Later, she spoke, looking out over the yellowed February lawn of the hospital after the snow had melted: "Lake trees speaking in the wind, whispering of all that is nature, and taking our hands, transcending humanity for the Divine. We walk together for hours on end, silent, and listening to the murmurs of water and chattering of birds, the wild wood and its core. My center is aligned with purpose; I do not stray from godliness as long as I follow the path before me. You, the Divine, are here."

The philosopher joined her, "I ask the deep questions of men and angels: challenging their rights to live and die as sons of the Divine above. They are sought out by me, and I request their true name, their true nature, and their lineage, in the tradition of the wise men who have gone before me."

"What do you ask of women?" she queried.

"What do men and women want, and what do they forget that is essential? Destiny, a young child," said the philosopher.

Ebony said, "After the evening is spent and the stars appear one by one on the red carpet, the night flickers bright and noir, on and off like a giant firefly, gold, silver, and the moon is hidden behind a cloud... I whisper in the dark that the time will come when I speak to a friend without the fear, lace my boots, and walk free like a dancer."

The philosopher pondered, "The train thundered through the dark, rifling the air at midnight in the street. I waited for it to pass, and the old heavy tanks of rusted metal left me silent and too alone, there in my automobile, waiting without haste, reading graffiti in bold stripes and colors."

"The grey rain is on again off again in the clouded city, pressing moisture against the panes, dripping from the trees decorously. People stand in lines for coffee, the talk hums... so they take the newspaper and open it and read some headlines, gurus of the real world," the naturalist finished.

"A gauzy papillon appears, her beauty glamorous, and disappearing star night after night behind the deep purple curtain. The inlay of gold in the ceiling brushed time imperceptible, into a dance and the notes turned chaos of a meld of slight symphony into order of the populace's ideals, and like a host of birds singing madly now it rose and careened around the room, deadly," he said.

Chapter 26

T he dimming light and last poignant hour now has almost waved and said goodbye, what sun illumined and held for power—sweep of olden gold on fields of rye, carving as in oak the darkening path: we would once more raise our chant to heaven, chasing down the solemn aftermath.

Ebony woke when the nurse came in to take her blood pressure. She then told Ebony to go to breakfast. After the naturalist ate, the other patients were given their morning medication. Ebony did not have to take any. The other women finished their meal, and wandered off down the hallway to play ping pong.

The naturalist sat at the table in the lunchroom and wrote in her field journal until someone called her to tell her it was time for her appointment with the psychologist. The naturalist and the philosopher looked at each other. "I'll be right back," said Ebony.

The psychologist was dark-featured. He looked unlike a prince of Afghanistan, with a Master's degree. He folded his hands, and let Ebony talk to her heart's content. Not only could he relate to her as a person, he seemed eager to hear her story.

The naturalist said, "Nature is a territory—a vast unchartered spanse of earth, whereupon I quest for knowledge of myself and others: to know and understand the soul where life flows deep, and nuances of human nature—the reason we came here, and how we will live. The animals respond in kind to the artistry of nature, its fertility, bounty and cycles of gestation and birth, the cultivation and harvest."

The psychologist said, "Just as there are many modalities of natural healing, there are many methods to recovery. Some methods work better than others, and all provide some dimension to healing that could not be offered without a holistic team. Some modalities of natural medicine include acupuncture, naturopathy, hydrotherapy, nutrition, dietetics, chiropractic, massage, blood analysis, and herbology. Having a qualified practitioner gives hope to the patient that they will recover."

"I plucked a rose from fall's garden, its sharp thorn pieced me and I wept—on my white hand was now a scar—if only to stay neatly kept. Twenty roses I have gathered, seeing not the wound of love marred, blood-red bouquet I have tethered," Ebony thought.

"I think I have tried most of the modalities you have mentioned," she said.

"I can see the issue here that has been brought up regarding your medication is not to do with compliance, moreso than obedience to one's calling," he said. "You are a naturalist and observer first, and that takes preeminence over everything. You must be true to yourself. Do you see my point?"

"I said a prayer beside the bed, that, in the weeping hour of lead, my spirit would rise, eternal—pondering the moments fallow, lessons learned upon the 'morrow, and every spoken word transcend while silence of the dead descends," she thought.

"Yes, I suppose I do," said Ebony.

"Do you usually find it difficult to go to an orthodox physician or take any medication when you're ill?" he asked.

"Fulfill my desires to complete, compose me, the red-haired muse until I am half sick of shadows. Create; make believe that I am immortal; act—the imaginary warden, you, real as the living blue garden," Ebony thought.

"I guess the path I've taken over the years has tended more towards natural remedies, health food, and avoiding toxins. Usually I don't believe in taking drugs of any kind," she replied carefully.

"I have a lot of respect for my clients: children, women, youth, First Nations, psychiatric patients, who have come to me over the years—some with mental illness and some without—they have taken the path of the healing of their bodies, souls, and spirits," said the psychologist.

"For I am the subject, auburn bent, of greater scrutiny than scorn rent; I am laughter in the heart of bliss, fairy token of the dawn's first kiss, try me, see if I am art divine, taste this stately dream of light confined," Ebony thought.

"To be truthful, I preferred to have a naturopath as my primary care physician and I was hospitalized involuntarily," she said.

"Don't just think the psych ward wants to put a band-aid on your deepest wound, and then send you home to suffer in silence," he said. "We have exemplary follow-up care."

To Ebony, it was a castle where she been captured. She thought it possible that once you belonged to them they never let you go. Was it a black castle, where one was a prisoner? Was it a white castle where one waved surrender? The castle seemed immutable, with an insurmountable fortress that was supposed to guard her in this life, but in fact it kept other people out. How could they ever understand that she needed to be cared for.

"What pillars rise majestic in time of your touch upon the easel line, what iron gate will bid you enter to that auspicious arc of God as center, even as we now pass in our dreams," she thought.

"Sure I'll agree with you," Ebony said, tears starting to form in her eyes. "But I have been unable to sleep for three years."

"You've already experienced some healing through nutrition counseling. Perhaps there are other natural modalities that would help you regain balance and be more centered. We all have a lot to learn. Some of my patients needed a helping hand at just the right moment.

"Here is what I would recommend to you: neurotherapy. I believe a lot of your distress stems from your insomnia. Years of inability to sleep can take its toll on the mind. My neurotherapist may be able to test you and correct some of your alpha brainwaves if they are imbalanced."

That seemed one of the most intelligent ideas the naturalist had yet heard, so she agreed to meet the neurotherapist. She not only wanted to be tested, she wanted to see if she would be able to sleep again on her own. This idea seemed nothing short of a miracle.

When Ebony got back to her hospital room, she wrote in her journal:

I have grown up in a privileged world: a mansion on Eagle Mountain in British Columbia, Canada. What the world deems unforgettable is the substance of thoughts and emotions, illusive as they are.

The root of her distress seemed to be a long-term lack of sleep, she gleaned, after talking to the psychologist. The thought of being free after years of struggle to survive the day to day pain of insomnia—which hurt like hunger—it had not seemed possible until now. She only knew the years of struggling to comply with a rigid solution, and the last few months of being drugged with no recourse.

I am a writer—a seller of dreams. Emotions arise in souls, and are expressed in words, both spoken, and written. One notion I have is that no one exists for themselves. As soon as I have the smallest moment of selfishness I am called upon to do someone a service. The moments on earth grow that I have spent helping others.

The philosopher said to her in the hallway, "I walk, now that my summer has gone, vanishing into the woods of time like a mysterious female fawn; treading the grass lightly, prints sublime of nature, leaving her memory, as the folk birth of each new season crowns its birch, magenta, ash, starry.

"Constellations appear one by one, minute spears of light in the darkness, their armor flickering, to now come oiled and valiant. Cold kindness pierces through the galaxy from loft high rooms where rain, snow and hail are stored, resonant with order swift or soft."

The naturalist said, "To autumn's crescendo, bow my head. The wind, a tempest of wild fury. The water moments, to applause now red, stream through lined leaves of mahogany in her basket woven in tree bark. Like the aching of an old woman, staving off the woolen winter dark."

"The pieces of my soul know intimacy with you in my spirit, when I am part of nature and it is part of me. I rise as the blue moon rises. I fly with the horned owl and the valley of the river is my home. I am now all nature, and she is my queen—the Queen of Ives, creating and destroying my heart. Tearing my fear and hatred, until I am like a jagged mountain face, or a stream to the ocean, cold and riveting. I am an open field, reparation my army, to go forth with forgiveness that will move my enemies to surrender," he replied.

She replied, "When reason and conscience are juxtaposed, when their meanings converge—humans glean wisdom from their true source, not the superstition of earth, or the wanderings of the stars, for they are far from home and must one day return to it."

The philosopher continued, "When people are connected to their true source, they are aligned with their own destiny, and fulfill their life's purpose. They find fulfillment in the simple things—their actions from sunrise to sundown are not mediocre, but infused with the precious seed of thought and emotion that brings life. They will not refuse the quest."

She said, "The Prince of Alchemy has asked his subjects to embark on the quest with their sword and mail, with a daunting prospect before them, and a hideous enemy called doubt lagging behind. Would we now embark together, the naturalist and the philosopher? We would journey all our days around this lake's expanse until we reach our last eternal home."

"This human duo partakes of life and nature, purchasing men and women until they succumb to hope, and begin the daunting task of raising Destiny, like a child who has endured the ignorance and neglect of this age. She is small and hungry, she is untimed and precocious, her hair is damp and eyes well with tears: yet she will take our hands and ask for our deepest love," he said.

Contemplations of Revelation

O true Hero,
O speaker of the play upon the stage,
O personhood we follow in renaissance,
O woman for whom we cast our vote,
Act!

O only playwright
Who wrote of protagonist before time began,
(quill, ink, papyrus)
Reach!

O landscape spanning thro the valley wide,
O heaven open to our wounded pride,
Mission of art!

O Seismic afternote from infidel,
O Music to the finest ear in perfect pitch,
O Ebony and Ivory upon the keyboard of soliloquy,
O word and verse that stands in rhyming couplet,
O Sonnet of resurrection from the past,
Great orator!

Part IX: The Next Song

# Chapter 27

Stillness was my contemplation, starlings pealed their veneration, the song of night, the nightingale sang with morose fervor, the nail speaking of my wound forever, telling of the writing paper behind locked doors, in enclosure.

Ebony sat each morning in the lunchroom and ate an egg with her toast. They served her a cup of black coffee with it and half a banana. She drank the coffee black. The television reported the news. A group of patients smoked outside on the terrace. There was a clematis bush that climbed the fence toward the sun. It was unwieldy and overgrown, but covered with flowers in April.

A grape vine covered the other side of the terrace. The shadows reflected on the canvas awning. Ebony asked her mother, Mrs. Velvet if she would bring in her camera. When her mother did as she requested, she did a photo shoot of the terrace right there in the ward, and called it "April View from A Psych Ward."

The nurse called her for an appointment. The neurotherapist was a kind and well-educated woman. She spent a month of sessions to correct Ebony's alpha, beta, and theta brain waves. Eventually, the therapy helped, and Ebony was able to fall asleep again. But Ebony knew there was more to her therapist's understanding of the mind. "What is the missing piece of the puzzle?" Ebony asked one day.

"There is a sort of bird that sings by night—a sweet and lovely song, the plain thrush that flies by the side of the road. The thrush in a hedge is the nightingale, and all who hear it know its moment passes oh so swiftly," said the neurotherapist. "It may be that your very constitution makes you more gifted with words," she summed it up.

"C'est fascinant," said Ebony.

"When did you first notice your nightingale?" asked the neurotherapist.

"It was in the night, the song began," Ebony replied.

"We pass by in the night like ships looking for the lighthouse to guide us. On the rare occasion we hear the sweet song of the night birds trilling before morn. If we let the song guide us, it would be to believe that our thoughts can have the lightness of a nightingale that flies out over the rooftops, that is cared for by the Divine, and never worries about another day," said the neurotherapist.

Ebony said nothing.

"This side of living must seem almost effortless to be successful. To master it, one must practice living not too bold, beyond our means. Then try to have small but meaningful thoughts. The smallest loveliest thoughts of the day are the moments when you will begin to harness your nightingale mind. The birds will begin to fly by when you least expect them, usually playful, in twos, diving and swooping. If you leave birdseed out they may even be regulars," said her neurotherapist.

"Ebony, one cannot ever be a singer part-time. If one sings, it consumes all one's life, every waking moment with the next song."

Ebony had all but given up her song-writing on the piano, but she remembered years ago when it was the most important thing in the world to her.

"To compose means to bind and to loose, to play an instrument is to learn and unlearn. One must quickly learn a new melody, and unlearn all intrinsic forces that would oppose it. There is a safety in singing, and the night is not so fearsome when pierced by even one song," said the neurotherapist.

"So were the voices of those like candles in the night," Ebony thought. "There is the memory, then the reminiscence."

"Childhood is like that song of the nightingale, the crushing sweetness," said my teacher. "Just watch an innocent child at a creative pursuit for any length of time. They must be unselfconscious to be centered in their task. The joy comes readily to their eyes if they be successful. Tears fall if they are disappointed. But if the night comes, and they are left alone in their beds, something remarkable may begin to happen.

"Instead of falling under the drugged ubiquitous power of slumber, their minds wake up. And as they begin to think over the events of the day, they become more and more awake. At some point it becomes evident that to sleep when such distressing things happen in the world would be wrong. This is a crisis that must be resolved somehow. They have already taken it on their shoulders," she said.

"How do they resolve it?" Ebony asked.

"Let me show you some examples: the first look in a mother's eyes begins the bonding between a mother and infant. Then later, there is the first moment of self awareness, when all of her very real emotions are not enough to stop the child from feeling upset or sad or alone."

"I see," Ebony said. "Where is the nightingale?"

"It is at this moment of aloneness that the nightingale in the soul makes it first attempt at hovering o'er the rooftops, waiting for the even darker night to sing," her teacher said.

"Where is your nightingale now?"

Ebony thought for a moment."The nightingale is stopped in a hedge under the shadows. The darkness leaves him utterly and completely alone. Is this the moment of song?" she asked.

Her neurotherapist answered, "The nightingale mind will sing, because the wise beings of the universe have decreed that he is a nightingale. He is the singer, and deep within his genetic code is the song."

"Is this who I am: a nightingale mind?" Ebony asked.

"You are a writer, and as a bird that makes you a songstress—always looking for a bright melodic side. You have a nightingale right in your soul," she said.

"My spirit is like a bird upon the sky escaping from the custody of earth, because I believe this is where success as a writer is found. Who knows, someone may make writers out of many young children next with this potential," said Ebony.

"Nightingale children and adults may be more sensitive than most. But to be honest, I will tell you that each endocrine gland in the body is important to our brain function. Each has a regulating brain wave. Writers and those who effectively turn their emotions into written words have a dominant parathyroid gland. The other glands predominate in the other five types of people, so I will cover them with you later in detail just to shed some light on the nightingale mind and how it is perceived by others," said the neurotherapist.

"That sounds intriguing," Ebony said.

"I only want you to understand that there is a difference between someone who just talks to be social, someone creative, someone administrative, someone who believes that everything is gained by hard work—physical labor, and someone who must write to correctly process emotions. The latter may become a successful writer, or experience repeat moments of catharsis, write journals, dip their toes in Rumi. Whatever the case, these people may be extremely stressed if having to do too many things in the real world. They would probably be much more successful if things only happened in books instead. Diving into a good book would be their virtuous place of choice.

"But they are not escaping the real world, refusing to make friends, or being anti-social. In fact, they have found their best friends to be most dependable and trustworthy at building character, and these friends are books."

"Ah," the naturalist said. It was one of those moments.

"If your childhood passed without you noticing, while anticipating the real world, you have lost one of the very primal tools that you are to take with you on your life's road.

"These are necessary to construct your reality," she said. "Joy, the first moment of unselfconscious joy when you read for the first time something that made you most you.

"Relationship, The eyes of a character and your eyes locked internally, and you knew—this book will never leave me.

"Commitment, I am in it until the bitter end. I will fight for what I believe in this book along with its dominant players. There is a hero who will win.

"So we learn that there are virtues and characters that we must endure suffering with, have courage to stand up for, and not compromise," said the neurotherapist.

Chapter 28

Ebony and the neurotherapist had sessions every week. The neurotherapist not only taught her to harness the nightingale mind, but also regulated Ebony's brain waves to correct themselves internally. She counseled her, to assist her in other ways. The neurotherapist taught Ebony that the other five brain waves emanated from the adrenal glands, thyroid gland, pituitary gland, gonadal glands, and hypothalamus.

"You've probably heard of an A-type personality. A-types are apple shaped, and are more prone to heart disease. There are five other endocrine types though. A B-type person is pear shaped, and influenced by the thyroid gland. Each person has an endocrine body type that affects their dominant brain wave," she said.

"Can you become a different type, or do you stay the same for life," Ebony asked.

"The determinant of which gland prevails is largely genetic," her teacher explained. "Your parathyroid gland dictates your emotions and personality type, even your gifting, because it is dominant."

Ebony quickly learned to compose her emotions in words, to keep her parathyroid gland dominant. Writers, songwriters, singers and musicians all very likely employed this brain wave to become famous lyricists and possibly had dominant parathyroid glands. Practically speaking, they made money from words, and sold songs.

"Triune God," Ebony prayed beside her bed, "the soul of our intimacy shift to take us in, holy breath and body, to a centered speaking and hearing token of our Creator's earth: vast naves resound, take the music of joy and youth once more. Disperse it from the church, into the street, where the poor gather and homeless wander. Light the windows of good Christians, be canon of the godless as well as God-fearing—those who rejoice o'er the news of a Savior and our redemption.

"Let the little children take hands on the eve, buffer them who are strong against the wild storm. Let the darkening winds of passing years not bridge our minds to regret the choice to follow you we once made when young and without cares or fear. The early Hosanna sung out of pure lips, the innocent worshipful bespeaks wearing whatever one had, coming as one was, bowing," she finished.

After a month of seeing the neurotherapist, Ebony's brain waves had improved. Now she did not need as much medication. Now she was hoping to go home. The doctors were looking on her recovery more favorably, and had granted her another decertification panel.

Ebony did not have a lawyer to represent her this time. She did not have a naturopath to represent her either. She decided to represent herself, and would try to impress the panel members. Her attempt was unsuccessful. They decided not to decertify her. After the panel, the psychiatrist sent Ebony home on extended leave.

Ebony went to stay with her mother and father on Eagle Mountain. She now had more freedom, and the feeling of a cocoon of safety made some of the fear start to subside. City of Roses had asked to use her story in their upcoming book and movie. She had several phone calls a week with Gabrielle, which was used as material from their conversations to compose her story. Ebony spoke with Gabrielle for six months while the book was being written. This was followed by nine months of production.

With this new turn of events, the naturalist and the philosopher felt inspired to begin writing rhyming poetry. It all started when Ebony wrote to the philosopher in the ivy cottage after a walk one evening:

At the forest's weave, the highlights flow through wafted leaf and glistening bough. The nectar of the flower, seeping breach—it brings the tide of summer to each sparrow, robin, blue jay—flitting bright serious beats, rise and disappear: unto moment shadows of the night.

I am reaching to each branch-barred heart, starting at the absolute of ground, now stony gowned and lush with fern, part with the meadow in its finest hour. The sigh of light will decorate and stream to touch each consecrated vial—the naturalist of rum-tainted man.

The playing tribute of another power, willing to now rest its fated lute, the whispering of our nature's lower threshold, keeping time with earth's still flute. In bold didactic strokes, and bearing chains of poverty, without this color. The dawn, its early morning sterling.

The philosopher wrote back:

Following the rustle you left of leaves on your way, as you walked around the lake: another day at work in science meant you categorized, labeled, caught, released, and I was an artist, leaning on you for didactic sunlight, setting promptly.

My inspiration wafted through the trees like the cedar oil of an old growth wood. I sat beneath the road-map of the stars— invisible beyond the blue; singing, I played my old guitar for tune, it rang over waters of the railroad trestle.

You were always there every grey day, all day, and never grew tired of life. The rain, clouds, or snow were never dampers on your forte which resounded, grand way. The mediocre never took your side; you stand proud, naturalist at last light.
She wrote him:

*Roses in winter, smooth as shadows across the haggard field: the
trees stood against the immaculate skyline, and December's
frosty breath was moved to exhale the crust of diamonds o'er the
ground: a jeweled tiara on the head of Mother Earth in glory.*

*The cold day was nonplussed at its fair royalty, shining
decorated dress of snowflake falling here and there, on each
branch, each broom, and heather, part and should I stretch my
hand and feel your warmth, it would be the strong gaze, azure of
your eyes—and a heart, beating now.*

*This tundra of falling snow, freezing ice, caught me unaware;
though I knew winter well, and his sister summer, somehow,
they took hands and appeared with gifts, as each season does
rival and relinquish its leaf, snow, blossom, fruit. I stand right
here, waiting to pick this.*

The philosopher wrote back, in fountain pen:

*The bright forged fire, aflame with reminiscence kindled
highlights in my chestnut hair and eyes, dancing with the
emotions unspent, now speak eve of mine, burnish this night of
swift Godspeed: with reticence we wrap the gifts, glittering,
and the candles on the tree flicker with warmth.*

*Here we are with the trappings of Noël's even, yet as singular
in heart as the saved, stooping to pay respects to a babe in hay,
wrapped in swaddling clothes, lying in a manger.*

Where we come near, there is a silence, a hush that suddenly we knew we were in need of him. O night of all most holy, touched earth right here: I opened my mouth and sang the old carol and you turned the pages, in simple costume, weathered by time, we never forgot the one who brought us here, innocent as Mary and Joseph, and we breathed deeply in frankincense.

She wrote back:

If prayer opened like a flower and I could smell its ripe fragrance, I would, intoxicated, drink its scarlet perfume to the dregs of oft forgotten man and child: what verse rise upward at their call? What child cries out and does not think an answer swiftly comes, reserved on angel's wing: nor too trite prayer, kneeling beneath a cathedral's reaching arm of light, and stained glass glow, song of choir boys in the nave.

This winter as the snow falls deep think of each word, rising from ground left fallow through the snowy months: the hard cruel blow of icy cold, that we cry out, preserve us now—let not faith be of dying might. Juxtapose our hope with healing, cleanse our mortal wound in this hour, let mankind once more sigh in song, attempt his dream to go beyond all that is earthly, now divine—we rise again, we shall transcend.

Chapter 29

The truth of life is sometimes revealed through myth, that we might participate with our imaginations in a story greater than our own—Ebony had cried many tears, and heard many tales, fables, and legends. To become one with the truth of the Divine, there is a higher calling. Start on the journey, the naturalist intoned to everyone— walking every day around Railway Trail.

The stony ground beneath the naturalist's feet became smooth, tapered off to a grassy ledge. She and the philosopher sat for awhile, looking out over the lake. As they sat there on the grassy ledge, day after day, looking out over the lake, the weather turned to rain. The leaves fell in a mosaic of color, and people drove over the dam and waved from their automobiles.

Ebony clicked the shutter, and autumn's finery became a print in time—Beauty. They walked every day. Bringing a hot thermos of tea and biscuits, cheese, and apples they ate every two hours around the clock. They saw the fashionable dress of the Queen of Ives reflected in the lake's surface.

Where the birds twitter over the plaid kilt of red and gold, fly high, soar and disappear—apple trees ripen their fare, from green to dusk. Where the winds whip the trees under the northern sky, there is an island in mid-river where the Stave flows down to Ruskin. There the mills groan and whirr, day in and day out, grinding out lumber. Beside them, for a pint at day's end, is the Shake and Shingle Pub.

The philosopher noted, "The Queen of Ives has donned her hat and purse in civility. The river passes placidly by in functional domesticity. She will eat her supper by candlelight—the moon, round and full, by midnight. Her night-light is the eighty-eight constellations."

They walked home, following the river's winding road.

Fall was always the way of truce before the cold— afternoons still warm, with breezes. The astigmatic sunshine filtered through the warm, rich, earthen tones and scent of mossy trees hanging over the water, as the naturalist and the philosopher passed on the wooden walkway. They were looking into the depths of a cerulean-green lagoon, bright as a dragon's tail.

The great elbows of branches shadowed the waters where trout were noiseless and invisible, lurking in the cool, swimming toward the lake depths. Be specific, specificity is your ally, Ebony's Botany professors at university had always encouraged her. What was fact and what was imagination in the field of acute observations; the naturalist blended the two seamlessly. The two children of art and science walked hand in hand.

When November arrived, the air became cold and dry. The naturalist's thoughts became crisp—she cooked potatoes and hung their wet socks by the fireside. She took notes in her field journal on the wildlife still present, preparing to hibernate through the length of winter.

For in the Western Wild there is no predicting the length of cold. Where an old Railway Trail disappears into the woods, snowflakes fill the air in winter. The silence of mist over the water fills the air in spring. In summer, parking their cars at the entry, families hike to the sandy beach on Hayward Lake.

Autumn is unlike the headdress of the First Nations People, colorful, solemn, and unafraid, she wrote.

In December, the snow fell around them in a blanket of white. Giant icicles hung from the rooftops. The lake froze until it was a thick sheet of ice, and you could walk to the other side. The naturalist took out her camera and captured it; she clicked the shutter again and again, filling the roll with winter's icy grip. The charcoal-black pilings from the railroad trestle, stark against the white snow, looked like people lined up in the cold—the remnants of where the train had passed.

They bundled up in hats and mittens. Ebony knit them both scarves in multicolored yarn and made soup from black-eyed peas, rice, basil, and garlic. They were singing a rousing song to raise their spirits, thundering under the rafters. Picking their way across the lake in winter boots, rimmed with fur, were the naturalist and the philosopher.

The cold was vast and gripping—a novel Ebony couldn't put down. It raced across the lake to an icy finish—like a crescendo, resounding from the cymbals. The symphony swelled in the orchestra pit from a dormant note, and her mind reeled: the flats and sharps—all penciled on a page once—were now elucidated in a movement fleeting and lengthy and prophetic of the black and white numeric order. Each note held its count, the mathematics of sound and fury, its brief interlude, and decrescendo.

"In the evening his face is lovely," the naturalist thought, "figurative, his forehead furrowed—and we are a two-part invention, notes lingering in the stillness."

The philosopher sat in his high-backed chair, hunger turning to satiety, their thoughts playing with the light and shadows of oppression and freedom. Music in their home was always imparting the altruistic. An honored guest, it wound its way—a vine, through Destiny's tree. It was the innocence.

Maybe Ebony was sitting on the stoop like a wilted lily, she thought the next afternoon—looking out across the way. She was listening to the creamy voices of neighbors, observing disparate people walking by. "Am I asking for water to fill this vase of soul?" she wondered.

"The base world bespeaks intolerable suffering and thirst, life begotten, ill-used," said the philosopher. "All lukewarm life moves toward oblivion, all red-hot humanity cries and pleads for meaning—creating diversity of color, race, and creed."

When Ebony was young, observing, she had spent many years watching people go by her window, including the window of her mind. Then she sat for several years silently in the wood, and concluded many things from nature. One of the most memorable things she learned was of nature being a mirror of human nature. She could only conclude this if she believed not only that life was created by an intelligent force, but also with a celestial amount of design. A doctrine of signatures seemed plausible to the naturalist, the natural medicine theory that stuck most readily in her mind.

Ebony wrote entries in her field journal wherever she went, not just in the wilds around the lake, or by the dikes. She happened to visit Minter Gardens one winter afternoon. Even in the cold, the gardens were riveting.

Later when she met Snowflake Princess, her daughter, Ebony reread the entries again, for her child was born into the world in the wintertime.

She wrote in her field journal:

The red brick path through the winter garden, where snowy shrubs bring a gentle beauty, are a reminder of what many have yet to discover. Star-like yellow blossoms of jasmine open, make an artistic bouquet—old-fashioned charm against a rustic fence.

Chinese witch hazel blooms at midwinter, abundant as a row of flowering plums in May. In colder parts of this land, the flowering Japanese cherry trees, fickle when it comes to early blossoms, now line the streets and sing from November.

Bronze buds and steel blue berries, white blossoms, the spring bouquet—evergreen viburnum. Have you ever seen a bed of white birch surrounded by rough springwood white heather? As winter turns the corner, bloom, its passing—wintersweet: stained purple flowers, fragrant.

With her sense of spirited wildness juxtaposed with cultivation, Ebony was planning her wedding. She went to Langley and tried on wedding dresses; each one was a tower of lace and tulle. Her widow's peak at last looked majestic. Finally, the assistant helping her commented to someone that she was like a fairy in the woods. She escaped from the decadent store just in time, with a rather simple yet effortless gown.

Her mother hung her wedding dress in the closet in their mansion on Eagle Mountain. The olive wood armoire was light-colored with copper handles. Her veil was placed in it wrapped in tissue paper. Thank goodness she had decided not to go with the cathedral style train. A small veil would do for a wedding up at Hayward Lake, in the gazebo, she decided. In the past, she had let her mother decide these things, but she wanted it to be fun and not ostentatious.

"For flowers?" her mother asked, inquiringly. Her mother was very good with flowers; she had always arranged them with finesse, and her precise touch. Ebony agreed to let her mother decide on the flowers. She sent her over to the flower shop to order the arrangements. Something elegant, yet simple, they decided.

After sending her daughter to an eating disorder facility called City of Roses, Mrs. Velvet could not turn down the mahogany roses and cream baby's breath. She had a way with flowers, and carefully dictated how each corsage should look. She did have the money to make her daughter look stunning, and this was her one opportunity to show her off. Eagle Mountain was a prestigious community of homes, and even though her friends might not hike all the way up to Hayward, she wanted everyone to know that this was a Velvet day.

Contemplations of Revelation

O true Daughter,
O true young singer,
O true vintage melody,
O spirit of the proverb's last word,
Intuit the rhythm!

O only receiver
of the three promises of the Divine nature,
(live, love, breathe)
Perceive life and death!

O black-haired onyx stone,
O white-haired mouth of rosehip,
Boil water o'er the fire!

O Steeping tea of herbs, infusions of the soul,
O Poultice of medicinal worth,
O Tincture of the master's hand,
O Ointment of the camphor's cool,
O Triad with the drum beat,
Reweave eternal destiny!

Part X: Snowflake Princess

Chapter 30

In the spring, there was the muted rainfall—the snowflakes melted, and the ice became clear green water. Mossy trees resumed their green. The birds returned and made their nests. Reparation was at work, and something in the naturalist's heart was beginning to melt. It was called forgiveness.

The Queen of Ives was striking, and even moreso the ice cold of a rushing swollen stream of mountain water. With liquid green eyes, and dark hair, her look was that of a fierce mountain warrior. Ebony had been given a diamond solitaire. Suddenly she was being hounded for interviews with the local papers. The jaded sentiment of the Queen of Ives melted into bloom.

Ebony's wedding dress was a gown of minute green buds. Pricking their way through the ground, like the needle of fine embroidery, were the new shoots of spring's eloquent voice. She was a high soprano—riveting, alkaline, and young. Blossoms appeared, stars on the ground along the road to the lake, burning fiery in a galaxy of ancient emotion. Filled with a pathos that would imbue their folded hands, they had decided to follow the course of their lives, and bid their happiness stay a while. So their heads were full of dreams.

When summer comes again, we will dance in the fields under the stars—they promised each other—roast corn over the bonfire, marry under the gazebo, fill the park of the Railway Trail with well-wishers. For the woods were their home, and the water breathed in and out through the windows of the ivy cottage on the lane, house of rain.

It was late May and almost summer, when the dream became a vision. Out by the lake, on a velvet day, their guests witnessed their sacred ceremony with the Catholic priest, feasted over the bonfire, and toasted a couple who would be spoken of for many years to come. The naturalist and the philosopher were now two celebrated artists for her photography exhibits, and their eclectic sense of style and new thought was envied. Unexpectedly, the newspapers hounded them as they left for their honeymoon.

Ebony said to the newspaper, in an interview: "I have never sought after anything on earth but the time it takes to produce a work of quality, a piece of art that will remain long after everyone has gone home."

They spent three weeks visiting Prince Edward Island where Ebony finally deterred from her nature focus to capture shots of the locals. They stayed at a grand old manor on the beach. She sat at the window seat under the plaid curtains and composed. She was pale, but her auburn hair was bright.

She spoke to the philosopher, "Our intimacy with nature in the wood could seem elusive and fleeting, the path winding away forever is costly, but we are committed to a cause deeper than this earth; cleaving or breathing the silence alone, tasting oneness or singularity. What fills my earthly vessel with faithfulness, like rosemary oil, poured out over my spirit?

"Take me by the hand; lead me in the ways of Wisdom. I will become a woman marked by character and flogged by integrity. I will follow the paths of truth."

The philosopher spoke to the naturalist, "Be free within. For renaissance is a force that can produce both good and evil. Yet, change begins in the human spirit, and anarchy will never find its root in love or hospitality. Your force of change will bring justice that restores our land. Freedom and liberty both invite the artistic expression that revives broken souls and fallen nations to contemplatives," he said.

The naturalist replied, "I cannot run from freedom; it has caught me from within and held onto me with fervency I did not expect. Yet many have died for freedom, and it is purchased at great cost. Those who have gone before have put freedom before all else, and given their lives—the highest cost. So the price of freedom was paid by an old generation for an even older one."

"We will become a free people who can die if the cause be great enough, or learn to write with great pathos," said the philosopher.

"We will no longer be in avoidance of the suffering of learning and education. The time we studied for a part will be worth it, immutable," she said.

The philosopher said, "For both poverty and fear have fed me, but I see your light, through the galaxy shining ever-bright, waiting through time for the coming of age of Destiny—for a young girl to become a woman that can lead a people. She is both kind and strong: she is the diamond that force has polished over years of reckoning with an inferno of doubt."

Ebony fingered her diamond upon her return. Her soul glittered in the light. The colors flitted like birds. Her community had embraced her, and she could no longer be thrown out with shouts of "Insanity!"

The philosopher mused, "The poetry light, burning through darkness will feed a nation—gestation resonating as its highest purpose, the burgeoning mother awaiting birth, as its highest call. She is expectant, waiting, and new life crowns her soul. Bitterness and unforgiveness have seeped back into the darkness and a baby appears—a reparation of lost years.

"Nurse this child of verse. Strengthen her core. Shelter the domain of words, until it heals where it has scarred, and repairs where it has wounded."

Summer passed, and their little home gained significance, as Ebony's mother paid a visit to the *House of Rain*, the Velvet summer home. Mrs. Velvet brought them a house-warming gift of a cake tier made of mango wood. They poured peppermint tea for her from the best teapot, and served coconut macaroons. Her white hair was tied back in a bun, and her visiting jacket, the finest she owned, paid them a compliment. All her jewelry was silver, as her brother was a silversmith in South Africa and sent her beautiful jewelry as gifts. She gave Ebony the pendant he had sent, just big enough to contain their wedding picture.

The naturalist and the philosopher were happy together under the eaves in the *House of Rain*. Autumn passed, and then winter. This time they had a new family member—a baby girl. The naturalist called her friend, Karen, inviting her to visit.

"A child called Snowflake Princess sleeps soundly under the eaves, dormant through the wind and cold. Sweet, she has large eyes and rosebud lips, snowflakes of love melting on contact with warm child-focus. Through the lens I can see again where I was blind, pique the interest of friends and onlookers, share the presence of this kindness to us on earth," Ebony said.

Snowflake Princess was like a laughing river—her small hands reaching heavenward, her god-heart, fasted in prayer. Her name was Ivory. Ebony stood with Karen on the shore of the Stave River. They walked along the path together, after years of unutterable silence. It was pain that had kept them apart. This time Ebony could see the other side of the river no one could cross. The fruit trees were stencils in hibernation, but they were there. She had only to wait until spring for the blossoms to appear.

"Now, we know life is different than before—for we are friends of the naturalist and the philosopher. Quoting mathematic and its theorems, questioning the greatness with philosophy, demarking the dance as choreographers, remarking at chaos and its turn towards order like physicists. We see the invisible, dimly at first but ever growing brighter," her wise friend Karen said.

"There is wisdom in friendship that prevails," Ebony said to the philosopher.

"Human nature has invited us to a table of plenty that continues through the years. Her wine is sweet, and her venison is honey," said the philosopher.

Chapter 31

The prophetic call drew them out of hiding into the open, walking around the haunting shape of an old lake with a Railway Trail emblazoned across its chest. Its black trestles were once dressed with steam, like a woman in a dream that a man can never forget. She might have been cruel. She might have been a brief interlude with romance, or a frightening waif with hollow eyes, a thief of time, or a mistress.

What wanton cold act could claim a man's soul for his brief posterity, for a moment's brush with manhood, for a kiss of steeled poison, over this lake which freezes to its brim in winter, solid to walk upon, and groaning beneath the weight of brittle ice. The Queen of Ives shed her cloak of fall's bounty, finding the lake's handsomeness disturbed, its peace abated, its purse empty. The disenchantment lingered after.

When the three of them sat on the point, overlooking the water, the Wanderer and Ebony spoke in hushed tones, hearing their presence reverberate over the lake. They put Snowflake Princess on the blanket. The grass was yellowed and grew in tufts beneath their feet; they took out a book and read aloud—wearing away at their indifference, swallowing the last of a picnic in the time of leisure.

Their words resounded over the lake. Two eagles circled overhead as if in witness, then disappeared into the white sky. The view stretched all the way to the dam at the power house. It was the dam that affected and regulated the waters, that made them smooth, deep, rapid, or shallow. The river outside their front door flowing down from the lake beyond the dam varied in its depth and consistency.

The naturalist wrote in her field journal:

The day captivates when the curtain of our senses is lifted, and we see into the realm of the surreal, a landscape of sun's kaleidoscopic metamorphosis, turning grey into color, wind-swept wholesomeness for breaking disease and homeliness, the unkind swept away by honesty and pathos, the length of days we have lived aching to see, and pondering at the gate of wisdom.

Ebony Velvet did not wait for an invitation to write, and her colleagues wrote too, with austere result. Under the blue moon, the beauty of darkness would always be the electricity of a word, the spark of divinity, the myth of reason, and the coming of age of a great many poetic spirits who usually wander free. It was a velvet age, a gilded time when those who suffered were regarded as dying swans. As Pavlova had once danced it, her starring role—Ebony knew, the dying swan was the picture of both prophethood and martyrdom.

The afternoon will wind away as we sit undisturbed, the bed of light will wrinkle our brow, swallowing us like babies under parasols, in the bright white heaven of togetherness. It's you and I, never tiring of the journey, walking into the night. We philosophized once that the lake would appear and here it is, glowing like a hot coal of purity.

They wrote to perfect their work to the point of publication. They also wrote collect their thoughts, as gems, to place themselves in the story (the setting of silver). The birds were a theme that repeated themselves again and again in their consciousness. Ebony wrote to her uncle to thank him, and immediately he began to fashion for her a silver bird. It was something of the idea of flight, and something her great-grandfather had done once for a flight community. In the same way, they wrote to be part of a greater community of those who wrote.

The surround sound of nature encompassed the deep blue, where all is swallowed by its obliging nature and ready boyish smile. We might strip down to our suits and dive into the clear gothic reflection of our shadowed eyes—from too much paperwork under the bright lights, where makeup runs and perfection is as the ballet shoes tied for the ballet, En pointe.

The blue moon rose over the Poets' Society where they now attended. There was a large moon painted in the background, and a host of purple balloons as backdrop. Karen took Ivory during the monthly meetings, and poet after poet read his lyric or verse from the podium. They paused for tea and cookies.

The president called the meeting to order with a universal appeal: "We must express in words what other people only dare dismiss. The world needs our higher expectations to raise the bar. Bring a civil conscience back to our community, through the history expressed in words."

"Conscience can only be developed through the history of nations, and the poets of Canada, particularly those of the Fraser Valley must have a voice," said one poet.

"What a historical conscience we have, dating back for centuries, and growing with each civil resolution of human rights. There is the community conscience of restorative justice, then the internal family justice of something that requires communication. Then the written word, including poetry," said the philosopher.

"When we believe together we can move forward, no one is too weak or too neglected, no one is left behind. Poetry gives meaning to everyone; yet we have been told until now we were neglecting more serious issues," said someone.

"How can we be wasting our time on something as frivolous as poetry, you ask," said another. "It is as if poetry answers questions that have not even been asked yet."

"Ask away in riddles," said Ebony, "for then if anyone thinks he knows the answer, he shall be highly praised."

"In the dance, I will be fairer than them all," said the beauty-sanctioned Queen of Ives, and the waters rushed, and the wind howled, and the storm raged. The lightning and thunder appeared from her white and black omnipotent face that a rock climber could not scale—a precipice of reason and neutrality. So she was, nature in all her fury: a ballet of time and romance, leaving rose petals for lovers, and dashing their infants like old dreams.

In the room of poets, Ebony could not see her anymore; her veiled threat would dissipate into a disguise, the people talking of likes and dislikes, of metaphor and illusion, of hot coffee and diplomacy. Reason and words would prevail over disaster, and the metered obedience of time to her call.

The philosopher leaned over and whispered to her, "Take me by the hand into the parched land of your soul, and let the Prince of Alchemy quench your thirst; for his heart is a cistern filled from springs, and philosophy tells him the time," said the philosopher.

"Unity stems from promise, rest assured," the naturalist said.

Later, as they stood looking out over the river that stretched as far as they could see, the mighty Stave, she was reticent. They watched the water churn, and then smooth past the island in the middle. They walked along the path holding hands.

"Kiss my eyes within your yoke, for there is a hope in the vast wilderness that me and my children will live," she said.

"Your unique observations of life and its meaning have captured me," said the philosopher with a smile.

She replied, "The vestments of your prayers have accompanied me through a vast wood to a place where the waters are cool and still. Here I swim in desire and bathe in destiny. I am the woman of the Divine, and you are my Wanderer, constant and rugged. Your bow and arrow have shot the bear and the deer, your hands have kindled the fire in other years."

The philosopher replied, "What I say next catches in my throat, for divine wisdom is what I seek, and the beauty of a nightingale singing upon the night sky at sundown. It is ransomed in the wood—effervescent and didactic, stayed on the promise that eternity will bind humanity to their trustworthy maker forever."

Ebony said, "I implore you, as the sun sets, follow me back to our ivy cottage, and we will dine at sundown. I invite you to cherish all that is mine, and hold fast to our future. The wine on the table shall be poured out; the bread shall be broken, until we are the broken. All that is our mortal wound, we relinquish: the fatal stab of society's guilt shall become his body on the tree, that olden tree of death."

"Last light has drawn its burgundy breath speaking through that shadowed copper tree, gathered toward the olden curse of death—sharp sword of fate could not now slay me," said the philosopher.

"I am host: both beauty and divine; all who rest beneath my sojourned eaves travel on, akin to what is mine," said the naturalist.

The philosopher responded, "With a walking stick, and compass bared, prayers for direction rift the heaven, staggered under the burden of care, took his black bread with meager leaven. Almost fell beside the rim of road, begotten of the music's power. Yet he will stand beneath his old load."

Ebony could tell he was a lover of handsome furnishings; while the mahogany and silver drew him, he was a Wanderer, and the Great Outdoors would always be his true home. It was furnished by the utopian hills and pines, by animals, fish and squirrels, and streams through the wilderness. His heart was a wild and savage place that he had allowed to be tamed by philosophy and science, as hers had by rhyme and verse.

"Drawn in life to whatever you yield, I am the fire and you are the flame," said the philosopher.

"When winging low over the red fields, a flock of dark midnight starlings came," replied the naturalist.

"Flitting sparks of flight in hour of eve, spinning their minute patterns like flax fragile quilting of the falling leaves," said the philosopher.

 **Chapter 32**

The naturalist wrote in her field journal:

*Beyond the earth, there is a crest of light—the blue moon rising,
a sphere, a song, over the solid earth, and silver wilderness.
Trees, decorous, now shadowed by mottled thoughts as the day's
dragonflies hide, birds roost and owls fly far away.*

She walked around Hayward Lake, alone, with the
whole day stretching before her. It was her daily hike that
inspired her writings. She had her camera slung around
her neck, her sweatshirt wrapped around her waist and
her field journal and pen in hand. She could do all she
needed to while still eating a Fuji apple.

*The brief interlude of night is no interruption to our journey,
traversing through the weeping galaxy of wildlife in this neck of
the woods.*

She reached the sandy beach where they often brought
Ivory to swim in the summer, and had picnics. This was
where she had captured the lake on so many occasions
through her shutter. Each season afforded its own flavor.

There was a bird's nest still in the tree that would be a young swallow's home come spring.

The sunlight darkened in the brisk day, the philosopher walked with me—naturalist, observing the way of duck, goose, and trout. Of botany I collected every leaf and flower, picked the blueberries, wild, round, and sweet; with the walkers I gathered my power.

Ebony paused on the footbridge over the lagoon, looking down into its clear green depths. Here the path was often slippery in inclement weather. She knew the forests well. Moss hung from the trees overhead.

Walking the circular paths in neat formation follow green and around to cabana on the pond, with peat moss staying over the blue surround, where the herons fly and loons call home; here is where silence grows, not unkempt, and beauty-beating wings fly alone.

As the naturalist rounded a bend in the path, she noticed a large tan-colored dog on the path ahead of her. Expecting to see his master in sight, she kept walking. As she drew closer, the dog unexpectedly jumped into the woods and disappeared. She came to the bend and there was no one there.

Young ducklings now follow in a line, hop into the water, winsome, soft as the early mist in the dark pine—from the

stillness take your cue, and loft of stars, stark, disappearing, in
bright light gathering its dress like muslin rays to sweep across
the room of night.

It was then that she realized there had been no dog. It
must have been a cougar, she realized. She could see no
one in sight. The animal had disappeared. I met a cougar
alone, she thought.

We found the way through the spiced sage wood—hand in hand
like lovers eloping—in the season where leaves fall and should
now fill the air with smoky hoping, permeate our hearts,
rustling iron, sunset, and sable, the outskirts of town like a gem
which sanctified the crown.

The wildlife on the lake had never disturbed Ebony
before. It would not disturb her now. In the way in which
all nature fulfilled its silent to raucous communion with
people, she had seen it bow to her. The cougars would
hide from her from now on. A heron crossed over the
lake, skimming the silver waters.

We ate bread in the dim rays of noon, standing on the bridge
over water—cool and sallow, breathing. Calling loon, a
decorative accent matter. Draw a concerto to its finish, weaving
the subtle melodic line of forest and field, this pond of mine.

The naturalist flipped back in her field journal to
yesterday's walk on the dikes. It had been warm, and the

sandy dunes on the outskirts on the city had drawn a number of walkers and runners.

I was a poet naturalist, and the philosopher was a man of meaningful words. The distance echoing back the list of species, chirping, croaking, toads wan, and Canada goose feathers trailing. We could but speak of light distilled green—factory of nature's unveiling.

It was at those moments on the dikes, and at the Power House Park with the gazebo on the lake when Ebony felt the Divine resound as an audience of one.

I pressed the maple leaves in wax paper and roasted dark apples with cinnamon. Mist rose, mysterious as a caper of fairies hidden in the woods. The trees were black etchings against a silver sky; and chestnuts were left where hummingbirds flee, and toward the pond, the shape of geese would fly.

Finally the naturalist got to the other side of the lake. Although it took the usual four hours of the afternoon, she always felt refreshed and thought the time well-spent. To get home, she would need a ride. She looked around, and bravely waved. Then Ebony hitchhiked back to the other side with someone who looked friendly in a pickup. He made walking sticks, sanding the wood until smooth, and gave her one as a token gift for her next trip.

The horsehair chesterfield in the sun room creaked with years,
amid onions and lentils simmering on the stove, humming a tune,
I stirred soup with chives, rosemary; gentle with the smells and
flavors, now to tempt him return from the flax field and taste
this fare—at long last, he did traverse and come in.

Ebony paused as she reached the *House of Rain.* She
stood in the pathway, looking up at the sunroom of the
ivy cottage. The afternoon rays glinted off the windows.
"Hello," called the philosopher. Snowflake Princess
played at his feet. She waved up at them, and smiled.

He sat in the fading sun with the door behind him, while I knit
a blue sweater out of lambs' wool—to donate to the poor. The
sunset was clear and fine weather awaited us the next day. We
went for a walk in the pines, smelling the oil of balsam, and our
hearts were heaven bent.

Ebony lit a pillar candle. The purity of beeswax had
always been her favorite. It flickered in the living room,
as Ivory slept under the eaves in her crib. When Ebony
was tired of scales, and the Bach had fallen silent from the
piano, the contest of verse began.

She said, "Where the river dapples under ivory skies
and blue herons rise from the island of tuft grass, I sat
star-gazing far off into the distance. The light was so pale,
I followed the dust path along the tired shore, where

fishermen stand in water up to their waists—here the fish are in hand. No need for a dime rod, when salmon land boldly ashore, silver, gasping, hailing their last breath here. They have returned to their birthplace in the river."

The philosopher replied, "Winding into the distance, the road—speaking of the dust and foreign jewel. Travelers too-toward real abode—a home, mended by each spool, in the distance, never proud; but the wanderers walk ever-on... minding their thoughts, whisper prayers aloud."

The naturalist said, "I walked about to the silver sea. I found the place where sand and briny foam, with the horizon's cool rank, meet—fish, all sunk beneath the salt, tiny translucent shells to adorn their graves. Storm, now faded on the final front, was in my navy soul's ringing naves.

The philosopher replied, "Sea—forever, I in debt to thee, destination of our homeless kind, clearest looking-glass to somehow see from sunrise to the end of midnight. Staid-marching to the peal of thunder, a trumpet blast that calls us, now stand, united as our time asunder."

The naturalist said, "The place I wept was in the dark of night. The elocution of my pain reprimanded my senses to dry ice, and I was a beautiful corpse in the death that is darkness."

"I would you but stay in the place of tenderness and comfort," said the philosopher. "I would but elucidate the times of distress have come and gone, and yet they hover

over the waters, mightily swaying like a fierce wind that doesn't abate."

"Philosopher, judge me first, so that I am not found wanting before the Prince of Alchemy, strip my soul of pretense and crown me with humility," she said.

The philosopher replied, "Walking in the seventh house, sea reticent, I find starfish, clam shells, and left-over stones strewn about the shore; lingering for docent tide to roar in from the deep salt, in moans of the ways of people and animals, both distant and divorced, making their way across a vast earth to inhabit the rough linen cloth.

"An austere tapestry through the Maker's loom: sparkling with the crash of shores, lapping the sand, wind breathing through the mountain's faraway doom laced with ice. This is treacherous white to all who can find the lair of bear and buck. The silver streams like arrows are shot through lanky wilderness. Creation's youth crying out to God in dreams," she said.

"The predator chases prey to bloody end, finding its food in the desert's mirage. The death of animals is far from the men's utopia of brotherhood image. I will consume only plants in agreement with the earth's force and timely peaceful judgment of all who with this poignant vow now enter," said the philosopher.

She replied, "In my interior soul I rest from life's troubles. I sense the bed of night drawing me to sleep— yet, I cannot sleep. For this is the time of the end. My heart beats a message that all will hear—I speak to you .

and you answer me. For our understanding grows with
each fault and every measure. Mute my very breath.
Abate my speech. Steal my home, until I find you."

Contemplations of Revelation

O true Physician,
O true cure,
O true medicine,
O spirit of life and healing,
Resurrect!

O only bedside watcher through the night,
O keeper of the lantern held high
(over the miles of sick and lonely),
Revive!

O white stone hospice of the dying,
O seashell mansion of the living,
Relay!

O Prayer before a patient's final word,
O Maternal help at baby's first breath,
O Prescriber of the remedy,
O Binder of society's wound,
O Strong and wise figure tried,
Renew!

Section XI: Ebony's Mantle

# Chapter 33

"Fly, fly with the wind, my spirit's shadow being. The herons rise over the lake and go back to their nests on the other side, as steady as the blue that laps the shore. They flicker and disappear, as the passing of times, haunting memories, and dark-rimmed eyes marked by insomnia," thought Ebony.

Being unable to sleep was something Ebony came to ignore, for the world turned, and everything went on just as before. The view would be hazy through the snow. They would traipse through the drifts on their walk down to the old antique store. Here, they could browse the selection of books, tables, furniture, and vintage household goods.

The naturalist noted:

Still Ming vases, still as wood were the porcelain faces, painted in blue and white-pale oriental color, waiting for buyers, or a team of Boy scouts to longingly look at them, high on a mantle, from a long time ago, still whispering art fascia.

Occasionally our eyes would twitch at the long appraisals. We would cough politely at the dusting. The insider glance of stern option and legend be told, Ming was of cost too great for our purses to meek afford, so we left with an old marble bust.

The places where distress is deepest—no slumber, no rest. Instead the lavish purple beat of a drum arrests one in mid-sentence and drags one down to the lowest hill, carrying away all the finery of freedom for a dual-diagnosis of slave labor and blackened hands. Where Ebony worked day after day to assume a normal reputation, once she had walked, head high and owned their rights, emblazoned like a coat of arms.

In her dreams, the naturalist tossed and turned, for there was a time when she walked free from the psych ward and found a nearby church. She sat in the back pew until someone kindly asked if she needed a ride or somewhere to go.

"I do," she replied, "wish to go up to the monastery."

The churchgoers surrounded Ebony in the parking lot and prayed over her for her safety. They drove her up to the monastery on the hill.

What they did not know is that she would be arrested and taken to Riverview, the old institution. It was a place that made even the strongest man shudder with fear. She would be surrounded and injected by the orderlies after the police arrested her. The orderlies then injected Ebony seventeen more times over six months to make her repay.

It was like leaving a tropical garden. The iron gates closed behind me, left me staring out into the morn where the sun rises hot and lurid over the desert no one wants for a home. The sweat glistened on my brow, and the dust cracking on our old hands. I did not mean to forget the day you promised it would all end swiftly: justice would roll if we bit into the forbidden poison red apple—the day our minds would truth crystallize and knowledge, comprehend like stale gods.

She thought, "One pearl at a time, the birds take flight—tiny notes, rise into the sky, home coming wintertime. When they are gone—a pearl necklace is all that is left of the black and white Mozart sonata notes. So I played it to the drawn finish.

"I was threading my necklace of tears, breathing my remorse—how to catch a wild horse?" she said to no one.

Ebony Velvet was left alone, staring at an empty bottle of Tazo in the old garden, the stone steps of Riverview inviting one. Then came the recollection of the photographs—how they hung on the walls of the City of Roses, like birds in flight upon the sky, black and grey, seamless in pattern. The smiles now frowned at the institutional and imposing brick building with new starched hospital clothes from shadowy mother figures.

"Wild horse you are caught in a pasture of wild," said the philosopher on the phone in the lunchroom.

Her horse whinnied in terror. She had once been tamed; now, she was unwilling to keep a rider.

"Is hunger a wild horse? When I learn to eat, does the hunger go away, and will my horse be safely tamed for life?" asked the naturalist.

"Just hold tight, love, I'll get you out. It just may take some time," said the philosopher.

She thought, "Here do not reciprocate in kind. Do not touch the sacred hour's own cross. Do not burn your bridges. Walk over to the other side and find your dream wandering by the roadside—without your power, lying right where it ends."

Here she stopped, observing the velvet bulrushes in the mountains of the sun. It was a cool day, and the trees moved in the wind. She walked down the path to the ever-flowing river. Here there was no Riverview, only a steadily flowing river of life. There was a beauty in the slanting rays of afternoon. A horse tossed its mane and came cantering down the hill to meet her.

Ebony was released from Riverview two months later; Mrs. Velvet had found her another psychiatrist. He was a legendary and famous man. He sat behind a wide desk in Victoria and seemed to be made of wax. He believed in orthomolecular medicine, in fact he had published over a hundred journal articles on the subject—it was Dr. Abram Hoffer.

Ebony thought, "I sing and I dance now, and say all the nice things they require, but I am not captive any longer to a decrepit system and high-washed old shower that would hose down our iniquities; the public disgrace, the inept comment, the inner contempt, the ugly scars, bruises of stigma, and social poverty."

Dr. Hoffer met with Ebony. He spoke with her about her experiences. He then prescribed her high doses of B-vitamins to heal her body at a cellular level. Eventually she began to smile again.

"I am a child of the universe and it ransomed back my soul, to a lake on an old railway trail as a naturalist photographer, to walk in the paths of the ancient trestle," she said.

"Return, O my soul, to the love of your youth—a home in the wilderness. A father's heart-beat rends the heavens to rescue his beloved children," said the philosopher.

"Clear gold, and reaching toward dawn is the sunrise. You are the humbling force we reckon with, transmuting base metals into gold. Our sin nature is in metamorphosis to become partner with the healing holy Divine that roams the trees and knows the ways of people: to repay evil with good, and sorrow with joy."

"The cold is transformed into warmth. The hatred someday must cease that makes us kill the child inside, subdue the distress, hide the anxiety, and starve the soul in a wilderness where no one ever goes," she replied.

The greeting of morning hounded them from within, drawing them back to the wood. There was no hypocrisy about the deep shade, the bluing grass, and the deep lake that engulfed them in summer and refused them in winter. They ached with hysterics over Ivory and her antics, and loved the hypotenuse of life, the geometry of purpose. The larks' song sparkled in new fields, early in fall when the harvest was ready and filled their table with corn and vegetables: moments, before eluding them. The naturalist wrote in her field journal:

My place on earth, I share with others. I am indebted to their care; just as the wild winds blow and ducks glide by in a wake of clarity, just as nature's gestation gives birth I have now come full circle. Snowflake Princess is my legacy. So the poetry goes, repeating its solemn measures, beating time, adagio in new winter, measure of the stars' silence.

She collected the photographs she had taken of the lake in fall and winter and exhibited them at the Kariton gallery. They hung from the walls in platinum frames, and people came in and stared, awed at Hayward Lake, in four seasons. Ebony's talent shone obliquely.

In her odd moments alone, the lake was still and smooth; light reflected on the water, and she dove into the green depths. Where summer had come, her shutter captured Beauty. The air was hot and stifling. They would get sun-burned quickly without hats so they slathered on lotion, and packed a picnic with Ivory on the philosopher's back. They walked down to the sandy beach and sat by the lake, eating and talking of the summer's best.

The lake drew the naturalist so she started to swim to the other side. She thought for sure she would make it there. She ended up swimming in circles and returned to the shore. The philosopher stood up and frowned.

"Don't swim so far out," he said.

The philosopher was now a professor at the local college where he taught English philosophy. The naturalist sold calendars of her photography at the local art store, did photo shoots of the green bluffs, and silent lake haunts. She also walked in the park with Ivory, or pushed her stroller by the steel-hued river. They experimented with millet, and made her cereal with goat's milk. They played with her for hours, combed her hair into curls, and shielded her from the wind.

"Where are you Beauty," the naturalist thought. Her heart ached when she had a spare moment to write. The Queen of Ives, in her green dress, was far from my mind. Uniformity was more what she sought; sitting for hours listening to a concerto—something that engendered the complexity of identity over conformity. Over the deep springs from which she drew water of literature, she discovered a lake—blue as an inky night sky—whereupon she dove in and swam. "One day I will swim across the lake and reach the other side," Ebony thought. Her strength improved each day.

Chapter 34

In August, Ebony swam early in the mornings, rising at six o'clock. The water was cold, and her fingers were numb. The wake parted in front of her, her figure trying the limits of her endurance. The waves shone outward as the sun rose higher over the water, bright and indulgent. Her black bathing suit was almost dry by the time I reached home.

Hayward Lake became a lake of literature, teeming with novels and poems, plays and short stories. It reverberated with story and practiced verse, rhyme, and meter. Ebony's mind whirled with possibility, and she knew it was only a matter of the hours in the day to perfect what they wrote back and forth for her second book. The rhyming and syllabic poems, the Italian and English sonnets, she pruned and tended, this garden of verse.

Her Wanderer had come home from a business trip. They sat by the fire, now composing the dark away as fall crept softly up to their doorstep. The creatures of the day rescinded. Owls and nightingales came out in full verve. What was once ominous about failure, now seemed the broadened possibility of success, and to Ebony that meant reaching the other side of Hayward.

Being a writer meant she was always doing research on the next field project. Being complacent as a ragdoll meant giving up, and she would never give in. The lake of literature tormented and antagonized them. But more liberally, it invited, sutured, and cherished them. They were in too deep now to escape.

The lake depths could not drag Ebony down. The Queen of Ives laughed under the book watershed; page after page seemed to map the shores of the lake. Fear began to grip Ebony's soul—what if Ivory had only them, her parents? What if being subjects of the Prince of Alchemy meant suffering in a way she could not endure?

The dread began in her core and travelled outward when Ebony heard that Dr. Abram Hoffer—her beloved psychiatrist, had died of old age. Her body had restored its nutrient stores through his prescribed supplementation of niacin. Her mind was being transformed by listening to the voice of the Divine. Her will was far from broken, giving her hope that she would remain well. Ebony had been a strong-willed child. Was her strong willed persona, what drove her to success, being mistaken for the rigidity of an ingrained pattern of disordered behaviors?

After Riverview, Ebony had her doubts that the people who stared at her in the grocery stores, or the family members who would no longer talk to her, was somehow unrelated to the stigma of a mental illness. People whispered behind her back. They deliberately misunderstood her, and tried to make her best intentions look poor. Stigma was something she had no control over.

She only hoped it would someday fade, and that she would be whole again.

Did Ebony hate herself? She tried to believe that she could love herself again regardless, so she would not be split right down the middle. She would try to protect her daughter, so Ivory could choose for herself in life. Ebony already knew to sow the seeds of spiritual flowers in her daughter's garden: the gift of assertiveness. She knew that she struggled against her mortal enemy, death. Every day, she looked him in the eye.

Fear of the soul has no adulation for hard work, patience, and the synchronized essence of partnership; it wiles toward compromise of ideals. So Ebony's mind would fall far short of her goals, despair, reeling and doubt. They were living in an old ivy cottage, and following the lake trail each day was her life's work—her pride would not allow her to fail at this new endeavor.

Malice, the fruit of internal conflict, and the pain of stigma were ever-present to mar the perfection of Ebony's world. The lack of rights in hindsight was adjourning the peaceful front, advertising her distress, advising her anxiety. The thundering of her soul would overbear the joie-de-vivre, but she was a fine-tuned violin, without enmity. Ivory was a gate she chanced upon, thirsting at the door of heaven, for justice, reparation, and forgiveness—like a cool glass of water, the sorry glass.

Ebony said to the philosopher, "We stretch out our banished hearts and understand the meaning in the Prince of Alchemy, his copper hands, the meaning in bitterness."

"I am a sandstone listener," he said, "and hear, the groaning of a world turning on its axis before Snowflake Princess and the darkening sun."

"When I understand the meaning in hard-heartedness I understand why I must eventually practice changing my mind—recalling to restitution," Ebony said.

"In the garden of good intentions, the Prince of Alchemy has a bower of hearts, turning each bud to blossom, anchoring the trees deep within the weighty earth. The olden oaks, still regal at dusk, daffodils turn their gold over the hills, and wildflowers pepper the fields with color," said the philosopher.

"Cleanse me from inside, instead of making me sterile with medications and white sheets from the hospital." Even if Ebony was clothed in only a gown, she would not surrender her mind.

The charge was to first certify her heart. She slipped on the trail and broke her leg. It could not have been her fault, yet the doctors did not believe it. She lay in traction for several weeks in the hospital ward, and her husband brought her a dozen yellow roses.

He sat beside her and smiled kindly, recalled the day's events, nodded at how Snowflake Princess was foremost in Ebony's mind, and that she would be well soon. She would soon be leaving, she assured him.

"Dying swan," he thought. "You spent your childhood life in a beautiful pond, and now your mother is afraid you'll fly away."

Ebony could not read his mind, but she knew he was unhappy. She lay still in bed and listened to the nurse, but what started as two weeks became two months.

He tried to contact City of Roses, wondering if they would respond. He looked up their number at home. The phone rang and rang. There was no answer.

Hobbling in the corridors, Ebony made tea for the few visitors that came to inquire, her friends, her parents. She spoke briefly with the other patients. Then she sat at the long table and wrote in her journal. Her pen scratched on the white lined paper.

The river peace, and the throne of time which doth, timeless, flow from the core to the extremity of doubt, so it wills.

In a light moment, I carried my inner child on my back, and the canyons were deep in my mind, resounding into the stillness. In a heavy moment, the jungle, a buried ruin, fires in the distance. The people were like night, and shimmered.

We sat on the sea grass floor mats, carving the branches and knots, the sandalwood, warm and reticent, stubborn and proud: those parasitic trees.

I carried my cross like a galleon on the Arabian Sea, a lone horse or twenty crossing the white sand. It weighed its brokenness under the wind, without a meal. The burning fever—a dark mystery in chains.

When my childhood, without an article or cry of dismay, vanished into a crimson abyss; like a man in a dream, I wandered near and far.

A last torch, I sent a note to my mother, sealed and posted, the brick building hot, humid, and decayed. But a nurse with dark hair and white skin sentenced me. It was a fine of sorts, to never love, or touch the burning tide. She said my lips were crimson, and my teeth, white as an apple—decadent red, the poison in my soul—venom stings.

It was a prison, where I sat in a dim cell, my money elapsed; my cruel boasts, but a war-time sword. The vanquished mind, bankrupt, reeled, where poverty finds its nemesis. The fracture of my thought was a hasty form, abandoned. I was too poor for a lawyer. We sawed our beds for firewood.

The naturalist noted in her field journal:

Still, my auburn hair and calm agile hands, a fragile mind of thread and patchwork thought. These timely buttons, still—a mahogany of doubt. Kimonos to seven thousand isles, remote and alone. The battering of a hurt, and abandoned field.

A twirl in embroidery and brown rice—one Buddha guards the halls of your soul, and unfeeling there is laughter.

A straight-haired boy appeared with a gift—the equivocal
present of chapter upon verse, of enmity destroyed for worse.
The statuesque book rejecting my frown: one million frowns.

"My book of poetry has been published," Ebony said to
the room of patients who alternated between anger and
blank stares. The nurse smiled. She surveyed the cover.
There was a flock of starlings, black on white. "Bird in
Flight," read the first poem.

It was not rejection that no one was there to see her
first published book except the psych ward. No one was
around to uncork the champagne. That was just how life
was. Perhaps when she was out of the psych ward, she
would be interviewed by a magazine, she thought. In the
meantime, she turned their glassy pages.

She mailed one copy in a manila envelope to the
president of the Poets' Society. She autographed the front
cover: Ebony Velvet. She gave the package to the nurse to
be mailed. The nurse nodded and hurried away.

The naturalist noted in her field journal:

The wall of confusion: where I end and you begin, what is my
milestone and my heritage? What is mine? It is said that the
oceans do not escape the sea, the fields overflow but twice per
year, and the hail is guarded in a storehouse. A virgin tower,
the hope of nations of unjust rule—of astonishing virtue.

Each hungry mouth, a promise of liturgy. When I kneel before the table, and rice is an alabaster coal, my lips are sweet. When my salty tongue tastes its greens, my thanks is but an orator.

The naturalist now looked like an activist, as her first book took off. There were two hundred visitors a day on her book site, hovering over the starlings and blueberries. Her cell began ringing off the hook—but when she went to pick it up, no one was there. It rang and rang and rang.

Eventually the nurse came and took it away.

"You are suffering from auditory hallucinations," said the hospital psychiatrist.

The naturalist noted in her field journal:

Each hospital child dressed in kind, the morning just a moment—when fabric, winsome sealed in colorless white, borne a vestment. One bank, in industry, and commerce an even flow. They would pay you to walk free. A warning was issued to the peace, and we are the medieval apple society, tending its gardens at dusk.

My pale visage, and pink shoes. An eloquent 1800's purse and beaded necklace.

Chapter 35

Ebony sat quietly on her hospital bed, drinking licorice herbal tea made from tap water. The philosopher had brought in her ethnic clothing from Thailand. She could wear it now. There was one brown dress that smelled of wood, and looked like a nightingale dress. She put it on. The only drawback to receiving new clothing was she silently believed her regular clothing to be contaminated. She would throw it out when she went home, Ebony thought to herself. That is what she had always done.

Ebony could only refuse to eat the mashed potatoes every night for dinner, and left them like lumps of snow on the meal tray. She thought they tasted poisoned. She secretly suspected they contained medication. Although she would not take a shower, she washed her hair in the sink very morning. She washed her hands constantly, until her skin became raw from antibacterial soap. The philosopher held her.

"Please get well," he said.

The mental health worker phoned and came in to visit, as she had received a complaint that Ebony was non-compliant. Ebony was pale but tried to be kind in response to this accusation. Ebony had always tried to be on her best behavior. She saw it as a mark of maturity when people could comprehend the injustice she felt with neutrality.

"Please believe that I have a civil conscience," she said to the worker.

The naturalist wrote in her field journal:

Children of the storm in a threaded needle, the hurricane unyielding. The memory of a wall that stood deep in an ocean of fear and hate. The watermelon, on the other side. I found you in pieces, the jagged edges, smeared with graffiti—red and orange.

Leaving the room without a moment's notice for the corridor, to tout some white note cards, into the darkness of the long night. We lay still; we were quite silent, behind the cement. We stood around, naked. My head was dark and oiled, and the holy cross seemed a vagrant. My inner child rose and died, vanished under the ethnic justice.

The simple dining room piano drew a crowd. Whatever she played sounded like Mendelssohn. There were white notes and black notes. They all drew together, then separated to their own individual solitude. The melody gathered momentum, then yielded.

In the armored hallways, our hearts drew blood. Unlike the others, I carried a handkerchief in my purse, and the meditation was over-easy.

The telephone rang. Ebony picked it up.

We speak in monosyllabic tones; there is infidelity in our mouths, under the open windows where we disappeared. Into a mask, I vanished, solemn and afraid: the infidels, a glut of security force.

Ebony poured potting soil out of a large bag. She potted the geraniums in the planter. She added the roses to the flower bed beside the walk. She stood beside the fountain, watching the other girls feed squirrels.

"I am straight and tall," she thought, "and I will not be vanquished."

She wrote in her field journal:

We are neutral; we will say no more, we ask for liberty. My dresses swept the floor once, and I wore my hair in a bun, the croissants of the Dashwood were hot, and my watch, finely tuned. When I murmured my condolence over the radio, the nation wept; they wept at the invasion of a neutral country.

The hospital is a green stymied pension in a crippled march, the grey grime of boots and artillery. Everybody claimed they were unhurt, their dignity still, and we faced the ground. The lily blooms, my world an opaque one. Could I hear your voice, for when I listen as my inner child, you are somewhere near.

Ebony's mother came to visit in her wool coat with big beige buttons that she wore for charity events. She brought Ebony two containers of soy yogurt and a box of peppermint tea. There were roses with pink petals and deep white veins in a vase beside her bed. A young child had drawn her a get-well card.

Ebony said to herself, "Every day, I write: a response of gratitude, and the poems are noteworthy and correct. Both in time and exact, I also take a milestone of photographs, my head turned just so."

The philosopher sat at the table with her and played cards. They spoke of the past, and Ivory. The philosopher had phoned City of Roses and told them that Ebony was again hospitalized. Maggie had reassured him.

"Juxtaposed—it is a time of desolation and a time of virtue," he said. "A woman named Destiny sat at the border, smuggling Jews."

The naturalist wrote in her field journal:

My imagination is bright-smiled, I knead the bread—your children, still young. Your homes, on stilts, are far above the water—the jungle, a plethora of ointments and oils. The macaw is calling its domain, the wildcat, a quill, scribbling on the forest floor.

"The burgundy of night is mild with stars, an alligator lays hidden in the shadows. Barefoot, the coils of the grave endowed you," the philosopher said.

The naturalist wrote in her field journal:

I remember the native woman with a straw hat beading jewelry in gold, blue, and sand. The earth in its tempest, was unkind. The flat arid plain—and my grandmother, a teller of stories. Ramona, delight of princes, an ear of corn in a mesa, the saddle and bridle well-oiled.

The seven sons and daughters of your race, conquer. Now, the browbeaten plain, and a lard tortilla was slow-baked over the fire. I know that in our pavilion, where the sun crosses the sky from morning to evening, season to season without end, we swung horseshoes. The dust settled, and the heads in the bean fields were unmoved.

The First Nations People had planted a garden—of gourds, beans, and corn. They made the Three Sister's Stew, and ladled it to the people.

When I sit in a room with you, you are not alone in a group of people who gave you birth but could not sustain your life. There is free bread on a table. It will not last, the fear—guilt of an older generation, who neglected to walk for miles in the wilderness.

During the hunting season, the deer is our sacred prize; corn our favored field, and the early sun, the sustenance of waiting for deliverance.

The dark-skinned children sit on chairs in the school; they can tell you what is wrong. They believe they should not be there. Your wood is uninhabited by the animals of your spirit: the bear, the deer, and the hare. The carpet has replaced the forest floor, deep in needles. The prairies are dust-dry, and children run in and out of doorways in the falling light of the reserve. But when I see your son, birthed and kicking in his own blood, I will know you as a strong fierce warrior.

My lungs and last breath were dancing like two maples sit at dusk. I memorized every word of my favorite song. It was the frosted garment of a wind, not unlike a mosaic floor in the parliament. There was a still and fragrant fury.

The Arabian Nights sequence—with some clear nail polish, we set you up to take it for one more night as Annie Sullivan. You stood on the stage; your light hair pulled back, your skirts crisp and ironed. The Helen Keller you know can comprehend. She can be polished and perfect. She is not mute or unseeing—her eyes are not unflattering. Her hands sign water, poured out of the sky.

"One generation at a time takes its place in line, and this one needs a teacher. She is unlike Helen, waiting in terror—without understanding—for a language to speak," said the naturalist.

She wrote:

The postmodern polyphonic opera in hysteria: what if heroin were in vogue? All six of you walk—you "I see France" photographers. Those soaring seagulls are quiet scavengers, encrypted, perched on the dock, digging for garbage.

They ordered us, put your handguns on the counter. One flattering musical after another times the core of multiplicity.

When all was said and done, Ebony could not eat. The others gave her their fruits and vegetables, passing them on down the table. She weighed only one hundred pounds, fragile as a nightingale flying into the sun.

"Enough for our sin," she said.

Her eyes wrinkled at the dust outside the window. They had walked up the mountain for groundwater. She had grown plants, and they traipsed along the shore. She had pruned the roses, she fashioned them into a garden of poems. The fish jumped out of the river. They had collected stones and driftwood, and arranged them along the window ledge.

The philosopher brought Snowflake Princess in to visit her mother. Ebony watched from the hospital window as they approached. She had put on neat makeup and wore her auburn hair in a bun. Her pearl earrings glistened like teardrops.

"Here in the hospital, many are not allowed in. When I can hear your voice, your voice has power," she thought.

"O love," she said, "that will not let me go."

"Ebony did two-hundred and twenty-two sit-ups every morning, Snowflake Princess," said the philosopher.

"Love is patient, love is kind. It ought not to be too fragile to be hurt—oh, to dance for thirty years, my feet, bruised and bleeding," thought Ebony.

Pierced for our transgressions,
Bruised for our iniquities,
Wounded and broken,
Broken for us.

Enough for us,
Enough for our sin.

It was dawn. Ebony was alone for a moment. She sang in the bathroom in her alto voice, without a quaver—and it echoed on down the hallway. The other patients turned over in their beds.

Ebony said, "I was imprisoned. I was numbered among the transgressors. To a solitary bed, I was confined. To a prison, I was condemned. I was executed in a psychiatric cell, given three injections for a sterile prophecy. At the Ebony Gate of the Immaculate Conception Church, I nailed sixty-six poems to the door, and stood weeping outside."

 **Chapter 36**

The philosopher read:

"She died under the surround sound with a printed bulletin. I had bought her shoes so she could dance like the wind. While the parchment paper told the story, she turned the page, writing with the ink and quill—her fingers, pale and dexterous.

"Wearing her favorite, the pink shoes—dancing with her, the memories unfolded line by line. Characters moved in time, and the stage resonated with lights. Eventually the poetry books and field journals would take their place, like a prima ballerina, center stage. I will always remember you, they said, and through the years wherever you go, think of me across the miles.

"Dancing, dancing: the corps de ballet concurs, bends, like a bird in an arabesque—in dark-winged flight from beyond the curtain. Leaving behind our loved ones, we fly in the night. The curtains shut the light—from a welcoming home to homeless. Nameless we wander, walking here and there. Shaken by the storm—looking for the lantern-bearer.

"Standing, facing the sea, the lantern bearer waits and pledges to align each precious soul with profitable destiny. When will they return from the place where morning gathers—beyond the night, beyond the sea? For the children lost, I know there are no answers. Still, they cry to you and me.

The philosopher continued, "With one ounce of forgetfulness, and one ounce of forgiveness, we go on—charting the course for others to follow; dipping our toes in the streams that flow from the heart of the mountain.

"Where live the bear and rabbit, the cedar deer, paneling the wood, the forest, where the oil of pine wafts through. We planted pansies all around the door and put roses at her grave with red bravado.

"The dew upon the field, and in the garden the violets leave their scarred and frail remnant. Purple flowers all about, floating here, there, in a sea of morning; a still-bright sunrise with a breath of heaven to triumph o'er the grave. Beating heart, that welcomes light with open arms.

"The likely peal of paradox: the blood rose shed its bloom upon the ground, its petals surround, now the earthen brown, orange as the sun. Its common prophecy tells of each crucified drop, red upon the noon.

"The shadows lengthen, and in evening's final light, the primrose—golden—speaks from beside the path, of younger year, whence then came a song that filled the grove: the oil of unity and promise, faithful—all of nature listens in."

"I also have something to say." Ivory stood at the podium and read her eulogy:

"Two cedar trees grew by the river, twining their roots deep into the ground, delving into the mystery of nature and the divine calling of godhood. The land and earth which speaks in seasons, fair and dry, or sparkling rain-soaked, is needed to grow crops of blueberries. The philosopher and the naturalist dug in the sands of time. Reminiscing of a former age, dilating the pupils of the past. Here, eyes widened, we perceive the truth of nature as never before, guarding our habitat, the human soul: we are moved when the wind stirs the trees."

She prayed: "Stir me oh God, in my perceptual being, make in me a pathway that leads to life, may I not be a casualty of the predator, but a harvest time that reaps in season."

Then she spoke, "I took a photo of the sky, watching its clouds billow and roll, passing into eternity. And the great wave of anguish beyond the blue sculpted my very form into measureless light.

"My skirts were the garden flowers, my hair, the willows over the pond, my lips were the red roses, climbing, my neck, the white swans swimming... I was Snowflake Princess.

"We parted with one last embrace and I stood alone against the world—one small dove—earth had abandoned me like a lost love. Then I flew upwards into a red sky. I landed not far, on the Railway Trail, and covered my neck in a small alcove. Beautiful as the sunshine resin rove. Streaming, ever streaming, tempering failed heart from despair to hope and faith—like rings I wear to ward off the dark in this time.

"So my sturdiness is a gift in rain, and climbing the ancient mountain I sing, walking toward the curse of the weather's nine furious storms, pitted against the grain."

Ebony's friends and relatives had gathered at Mussel White Cemetery after the funeral service. It was a cold day. The sky was grey and foreboding.

Ivory's grandfather spoke into the stillness:

"She was a fragile figure, but deep as the green lagoon where she had spent so many hours pondering right to the bottom of humanity's basin. Whereas many bowed beneath their load and cares, struggling through the renascence of life, she walked straight and free, setting the gemstone of flora and fauna in time—recording the movement of nature with her camera lens.

"If she is dead, then I am dead also: part of me recoils at the grave. Yet there is the garden where eternity lives, and I know Ebony is the gate."

The priest said, "What sunders and divides, what reveals and conceals. The concentric swirls of mime and passion ensue, for the truth of Ebony has entered into the Divine and formed a gate by which men enter the heavenly realms: all those sick and diseased with sin, shall this tale pass by."

The philosopher spoke: "She fashioned it with her imagination, and set it hurtling in space like a solitary planet, spiritual fervor, gripping the soul with Agape, dogging the philosophy of life with trailing vision."

He sprinkled petals at the foot of the marble black cross.

Ivory's grandfather spoke: "This momentary glimpse into the soul of one person's mortality and its eternity: a pelagic reproduction of earth and its bodies of water, and most of all, the Hayward Lake we knew like the backs of our hands. This resolution of the marring and the wound—all this Old World she leaves behind, its wound etched in flesh."

"For each day we walked, a song arose from the dust of the Old World and its nature. So we walked each day as far as the path would take us, and returned before supper, the cool flame licking the fish from the river. Then the nightingale would sing, and the blue moon would rise," said the philosopher.

The priest replied, "There was a fame that grew around Ebony, flanking her on every side—a determination to win, and the hard pursuit of eternity. Every word she wrote will stay here with me, a counterpoint of the three of you that formed a family. No longer inconsequential is this melody, but a legacy of the person she was through her own distress, sorrow, and pain."

"For I was brilliant plunder of the Divine, the spouse of Beauty: spirited untainted wells, flaming waters, weaving a spell of silent tableaux, as we were persons remaining still and silent in a scene. The unparalleled trail had punctual guests, visitors, and athletes, dog-walkers, children, and swimmers—the uniformity of blue on blue, and waves that spoke of nature's bias were a wedge between my mind and heart, witnessing only the chasm between myself and the gate of heaven," the philosopher concluded.

As the small crowd dispersed, the crescendo of life began again for Ivory. They were still unlike a Bach fugue, but this time the third voice existed only on paper. The two voices in the ivy cottage would converse back and forth, but now there was no third person to imitate in the ardent flame of a candle.

The naturalist had planted many herbs and resinous flowers, and the garden was still intact. There was a silence as the philosopher took Ivory by the hand, and walked with her by the river's bend. The day was cold in October, the loggers downriver would sin, cursing the undercurrent from the dam, and the white sun was swollen in the sky. Somewhere they knew—beyond the sky, where someone pours the water of our tears, there was a rock-stoic universal force.

The tempered fury of the natural world that had reeled and thrown its rider was metered and cold with dissonance; the ground at Ebony's grave-marker was

strewn with petals. Ivory stood watching the elements—
and could just remember her mother's green eyes and
auburn hair, the meaning of her words, and her slight
outspoken pen.

The philosopher said to Ivory, "The bleached summer
grasses, the wildflowers in her field journals reminisced
forever of years, and ways—the subtle blameless look, the
slight cook, the reeds in the river, and ivy, not undue
décor."

Ivory said, "But what would blossom, was a heart
under pressure, to make way for a world of myth. A
Prince of Alchemy would turn sorrow into joy."

"The transmuting of metals and the mining of ores
were spiritual practices in a royal dimension we could
only attain with caution, admonishing our souls. The
requisite for love had proved our own humanness. The
essential for the light of understanding had proved the
human experience here on earth. The philosophy of the
natural world became the melodic conversation between
us which grew into our dreams, our home, and Destiny,"
he said.

He had truly lived beyond beauty. He had sought
paradise like a child would venture to capture it through a
lens. Without a writer for a wife he would be lost in
thought; the ideas of women had long eluded him until he
met Ebony. He had dived into the blue lake of literature
long ago and now rose to the surface. In the cold water,
each thought separated itself as he uttered it.

"We could be selfless when we served paradise out of sheer brute will, rather than let nature dominate us with her clever and reproving force."

The hazed and clouded day dissolved the tears. The ancestry of their gift was bound in the numerous field journals that filled the bookshelf. For each day on earth, when a poet, was fraught with symbolism. A symbol was a sign that one was attentive, and listening.

"The search was always for paradise above Beauty—I will finally concede. There is a mighty war with the spiritual forces that reign invisible. Just as there is a spiritual path along the shore to observe what we had found and wanted more of," said the philosopher.

"Our Lady had sent us on a quest. When we returned, our besotted eyes attested to the glory of the wood, our love for each other, and the hearth which glows—there was a chariot ascending heavenward."

Contemplations of Revelation

O true Divine,
O true voice calling in the night,
O true light of day,
O spirit of saving grace,
Call me West!

O only desire of all my worth,
of the shades of my mind, and the colors of my soul,
(red, yellow, black, white)
Draw me North!

O primal source of all that heals,
O person that redeems,
Take me East!

O Watcher of the deepest heart of mankind,
O Guardian of the Sacred Circle,
O Talking piece with Eagle feather,
O Initiator of the story's power,
O Telling of the legend of people and animals,
Fly me South!

Part XII: Ivory Garden

 **Chapter 37**

"A thousand ashes scattered weep, descend into a darkening sea, as light that once was disappears from a sky that could never hold my tears," said Ivory.

Snowflake Princess stood with her father at the gravesite of her mother in Mussel White cemetery, at the foot of Eagle Mountain. It was the anniversary of her mother's death. There were small sloping hills, and the black marble cross, where she left a white rose. The shining street stretched by in both directions. Cars passed. She glanced up toward the mountain where she would spend the afternoon browsing through her grandfather's library in the vast mansion.

Eagle Mountain was where her mother's parents lived, and where her mother had grown up. Snowflake Princess had visited them many times. But now, when she was only fourteen, her mother Ebony was dead. Her mother had taught her many things and told her stories, brushed her hair, and made her hot soup. She had named her daughter Ivory Snowflake, in reminiscence of the winter she had been born. Ivory would never forget how she had been a young naturalist and photographer, an observing poet.

Every landscape held the opportunity of a capture, and the slight figure took her camera with her whenever she went outside. The moments of sunrise to sunset were etched in film beneath her hand. She would not take a picture of a person though, and Ivory could never tell if she thought her portraiture to be flawed. In any case, her father took pictures of people, and her mother captured nature in its most transcendent hallmark from dawn to dusk.

Her mother Ebony observed every leaf and flower, every bud and branch. She always knew when her Snowflake Princess was feeling sad or hurt. She knew how to make her happy again, with just a few words or a timely smile. When Ivory was still a young child, she had taken her outside, bundled in her warm coat and let her walk in the garden. There were plants, shrubs, trees, and herbs. Her mother knew each flower and tree by heart, when each one bloomed, and what it was for.

From the moment Ivory was born, she felt she was different than the other children. That only made her more diligent, to work harder for her grades. She had an internal vision that her future would be significant if she asserted herself. She might have felt this way because her father was the philosopher and doted on her. Also, her mother was kept in the hospital for a long time, leaving her to reason for herself. Ivory began to realize at this point that life was not what it seemed. Appearances could be deceiving. This was because, when the most beautiful, kind, and good person that you trusted most was hurt and mistreated in a way that she could never quite recover from—she could die of the brokenness.

Ivory, as a child, had wanted everything to be fair. She wanted good people to win and have favor, and bad people to be punished. It only seemed right that evil always lose to her bright powers. She provocatively employed her will to bring out the best in everyone, and prided herself on it. Christmas was her favorite time of year, because her birthday was in winter. She always decorated the Christmas tree. She put the angel at the very top, in her red velvet dress. The tiny white lights blinked solemnly back at her.

Ivory was almost certain she could transform anything to beauty. Trails of poetry emanated beneath her pen; she was to become a prolific writer. She lived under the enchantment of story, character, form, voice, and atmosphere. Unlike most romantic writers, she worshipped Beauty and anything it touched. Her mother seemed now the subject of a good art portrait, but also the personhood of a good poem. Her daughter was determined to immortalize her by promoting her books.

Ivory, at fourteen, took her father's hand at the gravesite, and holding onto her hat, walked bravely on. The epitaph she read was a tribute to her mother's success. The window she was granted into the human mind through the eyes of her mother spoke of the power of the will. Her mother Ebony Velvet had lived with unforgettable character in a world where cruelty and kindness co-existed. Her structure was never one of broken health. Her interior landscape was contained and measured in her daily journey around the lake. Her eventual detainment in a hospital, and her death, would only resound over the lake of literature.

Ivory knew when she was fourteen years old that the way to death and the way to life exist on the same road. All our powers of choice are employed at every turn. Every throw of a die was part of a board game she was subject to, and endured with much feeling and compliance.

"I'll never forget my mother Ebony Velvet," she vowed. "I'll never forget her ways of doing little things to bring symbolism to life. She has made me a writer forever."

Ivory's father wondered if this life ended with birth into the next life, but then he believed in heaven. He even believed in guardian angels. Ivory was still unsure of what she believed. The world was large and discomforting. Somehow the human community would eventually accept her or discard her altogether. At some point Ivory would know whether the healing her mother believed in was real or imaginary.

Ivory's father wanted her to believe more than anything that healing was more about healers than the local hospital. He knew what had happened in their family was an indication of the frailty of the system not of Ebony's bone structure or mind. He wanted Ivory to be free from any trace of diagnosis or illness emanating from destructive words over her mother's life.

Her father took her to a naturopath. Her mother Ebony had visited the naturopath with her husband the philosopher many times. The tall man was kind as he explained to Ivory something he thought she should know. He leaned forward.

"My philosophy is simple," he said. "To harness the earth in all its curative powers is to harness the energy of healing. Nature's medicine chest includes the herbs, enzymes, tinctures, homeopathics, vitamins and minerals that restore electromagnetic balance."

"Your life energy is like a river," he continued, "and removing the obstacles to your health is the role of natural medicine. I help people learn to shape their consciousness to empower their choices, make new habits, find healthier comforts in life, and move you from inability and illness to wellness and healing.

The naturopath's words made him somehow no longer a stranger, but a friend. He had studied many years to enter the field of medicine. He had wanted to treat Ebony from a natural perspective. He had even visited her in the hospital, and attended her first panel review hearing.

"You have endured stress, and painful loss," he said, "but I encourage you to begin the journey today towards life."

The sunlight became divided through the wide panes of the naturopath's office. Ivory's hair of gold was lit to the color of a candle's flame. She eyed the many bottles and vials of natural medicine. Her mind reeled as she sought to comprehend the naturopathic doctrine from the doctor's words.

Ivory could never walk away from her mother's legacy; she could only confirm and impress it upon others. More than anything she wanted to tell the story of her mother's life, despite the suffering and pain. But the years her mother spent in and out of the psych ward battling a mental illness made it hard for Ivory to hold on. She reviewed the facts in her young mind.

The naturopath had asserted there was nothing wrong with his patient in her first panel review. Her mother had been decertified; she had even paid him a thousand dollars for his time. His influence and education held weight in this frightening place of isolation. Surely there was a way to see through the conflict in her mother's mind to healing.

Her mother's writing was an influence on a small town that could not be discounted. Her work had been published in two books before her death, alerting the citizens of the Fraser Valley that Ebony was an accomplished poet and storyteller. Some of them were furious. How could such a mystical and accomplished poet been put in a psych ward against her will? That made the turn of events look like a modern day witch hunt. Her books were covered in the local newspapers. Many flocked to the bookstores. Was it possible that her true story was silent—that it rested solely with the philosopher and Snowflake Princess?

The newspaper reviews had been positive. "This vivid capture of the soul is a window into the human mind," the Times noted. "It is a testament to survival and the redemptive power of suffering. It portrays the members of family in a healing relationship and believes in the existence of support and community."

"When we see our frailty, our humanness in our world today, and witness the suffering of others, do we turn away, or come alongside the person so they can recover and heal?" wrote the Mission Record.

"Do we want to become better people for what we have gone through? We must choose how we will respond," wrote the Abbotsford News.

Her father affirmed to her also, "Your mother's verse portrays the inner child and the dilemma of the will before her death—affecting her family and those around her. Her life and legacy, however, pay tribute to the person she was. She chose to live life to the fullest, and her story grips us."

Ivory opened her mother's field journal, one of dozens. Her mother's life as a naturalist spoke of her commitment to observation over changing things. She consistently observed both nature and people. She might have been unwilling to change anything about herself had she not been pressed to the limit.

At some point, healing, for her mother, became about what she should change, and what she should do differently moreso than what should stay the same. There was a sense of "metanoia" being the far opposite of her illness, for it involved changing one's mind. Mental illness seemed rooted in a rigid way of thinking that was unwilling to change. The treatment of mental health patients should advance with natural medicine, this seemed logical.

It was one of the healers Ebony had encountered during her stay at the hospital who had taught her the language of the nightingale, a song in the night. The neurotherapist knew about the six brain waves that regulated human thought. She had employed her knowledge and research to retrain Ebony's thinking from despair to hope. It was the nightingale constitution in her mother that sang so sweetly and flawlessly. It was this always looking for the next song.

 # Chapter 38

It was not uncommon to see a young poet, with her hair in braids, writing in the garden under the blooms. Snowflake Princess was barely a teenager, but was a writer unlike her mother. She was only ten when her mother died, but her written work was a tapestry of thoughts, emotions, and colors in words. How can a child give birth to her mother? Yet this seemed the case.

Her father noted, "The minutes tick by when absolution becomes us, and the young poet is a flowering blossom that falls to the ground, pink and fragrant—papering the earth with spring, conducting the descant of a thousand voices, docile to the wind's wrath against the trees, their branches whip shamelessly: their leaves are new and egg-shell green, and the earth holds herself steady and looks the future in the eye."

His daughter wrote:

While pansies dutifully line the walk, their eyes roaming to the sky and back, small birds dart into the white sun—winsome in their thought-bound flight.

The philosopher wrote back:

I sit beneath the leaves of the magnolia tree writing of the gestation of spring to summer, and the late light's rays fall across my page, illuminating each word, scrawled in fear of forgetting the past, etched in ink for a brighter time, for a better world, reminiscent of when the sap of life was still young and dreams not far from days of youth—when roses were yet buds, and birds pecked through eggs to hatch.

The philosopher had been asking the deep questions of men and angels for most of his career as a professor. He sat at his wooden desk in the classroom and his assignments were piercing.

He asked men, "What is your spiritual self?"

He awaited their careful response.

The philosopher believed in having another language with which to understand his soul, and it was verse. He taught English philosophy at the local college when he was not taking walks by the river with Ivory. He himself would think outside the box as they conversed in poetry, just as he had done with Ebony.

"What will you live for and what will you die for?" he asked his students.

He was unwilling to let them be cowardly human beings, but demanded they consider the cost to be people of purpose and valor. At least live for something you would die for, he thought openly. And his students respected his opinions. His daughter was raised to express her viewpoints well in words. Ivory was able to construct an essay of ideas and validate them.

"Is this all a dream, that mother is gone?" Snowflake Princess asked one day.

"What an interesting question," said the philosopher. "I suppose that one day we will see her again, and the world beyond will be more real than this one. That is why this world passes like only a dream."

"Father, did she commit suicide?" Ivory asked.

"Well in some ways her condition would lead you to believe that. But I can't just end my logic there. I don't think they really know how she died. It might have been from a drug overdose in the hospital."

"I will be a writer too," said Ivory. "Dad, here is a song I wrote," she said, glancing shyly at his handsome face.

"I have a dream that I could see you again. Arms stretched to sky, a smile enraptured at my sight. Love, like the night's great expanse, star-filled wide—breathing each song from my heart to your heart."

When she was still a child, Snowflake Princess took notes on cards, and pasted together words, until she could make her own poems. She was not afraid of words, as she was not afraid of death. She knew some people used the strongest words in the English Dictionary to express their emotions, and even knew some wished for things they did not mean to.

She gazed in the mirror. Her blond hair and clear porcelain visage stared back at her, unblinking. She looked nothing like her mother or father, but instead resembled her grandmother. Her grandmother had had white blonde hair when she was young.

She did not forget the library on Eagle Mountain filled with books, the desk with plume and inkwell, and her yearning to be included among the volumes of the poets. She took up her pen every day, and practiced its powers. She verily imagined herself into being. She thought a writer was someone that people respected, while at the same time treated everyone equally. Every person was free to read, and no book barred the door. In this way, a book would never discriminate, but reveal its message to all who searched it out.

Ivory was often working on her novels outside on the school ground, recoiled at the thought of human contact, and was as reclusive as a being could be. It was Ivory, sitting in the school library at lunchtime who prevailed over the other children with a diligence not her age, writing her characters out in longhand, describing their adventures and measures of success and failure. She was simply "Ivory" to her classmates. She began to grow like a spring lime shoot against the schoolyard wall of brick, and then, instead of fading as she became older, grew bolder and more accentuated, until she was wisteria covering the entire wall.

She varied between the silence of a well-kept secret and its sunburst of nostalgia; somewhere in the range of neutral was her hidden palette. Ivory kept her distance from others, guarding her family's privacy and her mother's legacy. Yet, Ivory was a people watcher; she did watch them, unlike her mother had, learning the careful powers of observation. She practiced the ethics of cooperation, advocating her whims and fancies with collaboration. She was a problem solver and did so on paper, wanting things to work out well for everyone.

The philosopher asked himself frequently, "What is the meaning of this symbol, or this sign?" for he loved to interpret both dark speech and dreams.

When tragedy struck his own household, his questioning suddenly redefined the meaning in suffering. There was both poetry and symbolism. What is a symbol unless it carries both a significance of its own, and means something to you personally? "Life-changing martyrdom is never kind," he thought, "but rather something one tries to escape if at all possible, and survive gracefully."

"Does it happen to us to make us more acceptable to the divine forces of this universe," he wondered. "Does it question our values?"

Beyond anything Ivory could imagine, was that she felt alone as a teenager, without her mother to sympathize with her. She wondered what her mother would say and do in almost every situation. When she was faced at school with the other girls' taunts, she was not afraid. She knew other teenagers did and said things both kind and cruel. Some days one, and some days the other. She was not hesitant to be both practical and severe. She thought these girls should be stopped, but she usually could not think of a response.

"The world is my art gallery, don't make it your trash can," she replied to them one day.

From that moment on, Ivory held her own. Her friends rallied around her, rather than eye her from a distance. Ivory was a popular girl now, for she was both beautiful and skilled as a writer. Her verse was poignant and lyrical and won several blue ribbons in literature contests.

Ivory could recall that her mother had suffered against her will. She remembered that she had been detained several times in the hospital without her understanding why. Her mother had been cruelly told, when she wanted to leave, that she showed no insight into her disease. Was it Ivory who now had a balanced view of both sides of the human puzzle? Ivory could understand that the doctors wanted to convince her grandparents that Ebony suffered from psychosis, and was diagnosed with a mental illness.

Her mother would never listen to this medical jargon.

Something deeper was propelling her into the Divine and its true nature. She believed her poetry had purpose and meaning if not in this life, than in the next. She raised her daughter to be both aware and engaged with life in all its forms.

Her mother had asked the philosopher one day: "Should I ever be kept in a hospital. Would I leave my daughter Ivory and the simple life at Hayward Lake I love behind?"

"The simple life is the best the Divine has to offer, for we are available to his trials and his mercies," he responded.

"You are both too important to lose, Nightingale."

Chapter 39

Ivory sat in the garden most days, when the weather was fair. She was a young woman who was meant to study, and she studied nature as much as human nature. Life was her masterpiece. She practiced the art of plays on words. She rehearsed a recitation of Wordsworth. She pined over verses of her own. When she thought a poem was finished she read it to the philosopher.

"What dry and brittle blessing crept o'er the ground, sharpening every thought, my mind, once a parched desert, white as an elephant's ivory; the sun rose, far away—elegant in an orange robe—lighting this small world to flame."

For after all she had been through, Ebony's thoughts remained. Her mother had once said, "Words have power behind them. When we speak, we are imparting either healing balance or negativity. It is important that we harness the power of words to begin to heal the human soul, our nation and our people groups worldwide.

"Our words can heal and our words can kill. When our words heal, we become restorers of the human condition to what it was meant to be. People are free to realize their full potential. When our words kill, people fall into destructive patterns, thoughts, and habits, leading to their eventual downfall."

"I agree with you," had said the philosopher, for he was teaching a course at the college on restorative justice. "In order to be a free society that provides both justice and the resolution of ills, we must have access to restorative justice."

"What does this entail?" her mother had asked.

"Restorative justice is about using words to heal, in a group context. It is also about listening, and guarding the circle. Restorative justice should be played out in the realm of natural medicine, as these two complement each other, and speak of each other's power and presence in the world. Without the practice of restorative justice, we would exist in a world that was perhaps fair. When it is employed, people's thinking turns a corner.

"Let us use this tool we gain to begin to repair the damage that society has done in influencing our choices, behaviors, and thinking. Where the influence of the mass market, consumerism, and advertising was incorrect, we correct it now. We play out a civil conscience in the human soul as profitable not in dollars and cents, but in positive outcomes and healing modalities that can change the earth into a safe place to be. A historical conscience creates safe people to be around, and encourages the best in everyone to flourish," he finished.

Her mother then smiled.

She quoted, "And the light danced in lost sky pattern, shifting over the grey sidewalk, where children skipped, stopped before your lectern: quiet to their inner music there and the breeze carried your solemn voice reading word upon word as keeper of a truce to rise above the noise."

Ivory, upon overhearing their conversation, laughed. Her father was jealous of everything that had stolen her mother's attention until then—and he used it to his advantage. Now she continued to read him her verse:

"The turrets of time glistened in the morn, soaking up the chants of followers, faced east, praying and bowing, in worshipful pose; yet their hearts beat with the current of the last prophecy.

"Now, dark ears straining to catch a word of its subtle verse, hear. Wind and moon, sun and stars, lingering still—bathe the oceans in a dull glow, birth their salty roar, cantering far away to where the skies bend."

"Aha!" he answered. "Spoken like a true author. Your mother would be proud."

She smiled slowly.

"Do you realize," he said to her now comprehending ear, "our family is unlike a fugue—a counterpoint composition is a piece with three voices, each repeating the same melodic line."

"Do you mean the composer Bach?" she asked.

"Well yes, he was the master of counterpoint," said her father. "You have repeated the legacy of your mother's writing, reminding me of that very skill in music."

"The art of writing and the painting of word pictures are two skills to be mastered for the creation of authentic poetry. This is a point of discussion for the avid learner and a point of advancement for the skilled writer. Each poet is different and their life experiences may vary greatly, yet they all have one thing in common—they are able to harness the power of words to express thought, emotion, and symbolism.

"Ordinary life is fraught with meaning, sometimes unspoken. Ordinary people sometimes take on extraordinary challenges, in spite of the odds. Ordinary objects can have sentimental value, and are deeply treasured. When woven together, the ordinary objects and experiences of life create a tapestry of color. Everyone has a tapestry to create, and art is a multi-faceted gem of finely tuned mediums that require a lifetime of practice.

He continued, "Unlike learning a musical instrument, one must practice using words in rich and familiar ways daily. You keep a regular journal of your most poetic thoughts and feelings, words, and word pictures. I have a dictionary or thesaurus on hand to expand my vocabulary. Then muse over other poets, in books, libraries, or online. Find your favorite writers, and hone your inspiration to create new material. If you accomplish with your gifting it will have meaning and purpose, and may even become your future profession.

"In learning counterpoint poetry, three voices are studied. In poetry, they are atmosphere, voice or character, and form or genre. These three voices each

have their own essence in the creation of a unique poem
that captures the mind and imagination of the reader.
Think of how a poem sounds out loud. Think of how it
looks on a page. What is the desired end result of your
word painting?" he said.

"Wow, dad, I had no idea," said Snowflake Princess.

He responded, "Here is one of my favorite poems,
for you:"

White rose of Yorkshire, in the garden of the lamb,
you are milky and smooth with eighteen petals,
and each one will open when you bloom
from reticent heart to stem.
With hands of fine porcelain
my dark daughter is beautiful still.

Princess in the garden of her youth,
disavowing all that would malign
the stately station of her precious kind.
She sits alone on the stone bench
where doves flutter sweetly and there breathes
of all immortal powers, virtues.

Kindness shall never leave a woman destitute,
and Chivalry shall find her
on the grey stormy mountain front;
Patience is her fine embroidery,
Prudence cooks with her flowered apron,
Charity shall keep The Porcelain Rose.

"That's one of my own," he said.

"I have one for you," she said.

"I am breathless at the white immortality of roses on a grave, and the smooth blossom of the bud from molten center. I am riveted by the core of color that captures a lover's soul until he sends a dozen red roses. I am captured by the intimacy of nature's kiss on this Shakespearean woman, growing in a garden's bliss.

"I am stolen, like a thief who claims one bloom as his own after sundown; plucking its fainted red drop. I am bartered for in a market of reckoning, traded for all the wealth of one man and his pocket of silver. I am wanted more than anything on earth, below heaven, for a fragrance, celestial and divine.

"The velvet dusty rose or rich wine, I crush the petals until they turn to oil. In a magnificent palace, they would be my bed—their crimson perfume, my pillow. Where there is a rose, true beauty emanates and wisdom abounds, scarlet and ivory crowns—and I am saturated by their golden kiss, haunting, winsome, and royal."

Her father told her one day, "I was walking down the winding road in the mountains of the sun, watching the bright dance of spare light and shadow over the fields. An old woman came walking along, met me there, and asked for a poem. 'Recite it out loud,' she asked.

"I was silent for a moment, and then saw the power of the poem was in its gestation from mind to page, and its birth from author to listener. Then it took flight and was comforting to humanity and its rickshaw. Nature bowed to theology in each verse where poverty assuaged the ills of wealth, and made there present a circle of which I was guardian, and the keeper of silence, where there were words, now spoken with permission," said her father.

"Oh," Snowflake Princess was silent. The conversation had given her food for thought. She had pondered her mother, and now she pondered an elderly woman in the mountains who had made a simple request.

 **Chapter 40**

The balmy season came, Ivory wrote, *and the rain was fragrant, scented, sweet; its ambrosial ylang ylang hung over the vestiges of religion in a tower of time.*

Redolent, came the breeze of the new spiritual awakening—ardent and blazing, fiery glowing. Michelangelo woke to be vehement from impassive, flaming forehead from cool tempered.

I seek to touch both artisan and master. The Maestro featured his virtuoso while the orchestra pit was cavalier; the scholar took from his arsenal Bach.

My imperial art, lofty in the heavens—the clouds summon their blue against silver—the cherubs converse with nations and peremptory, play a dominant Sistine chord.

She had turned the pages of her mother's worn field journals many times. The ink was stained with tears. Now she took another book of Ebony's from the shelf. Snowflake Princess stared at the page. The words of the book read, "Love never dies."

"I cannot believe I have found an author who knows exactly how I feel," she thought of Emily Brontë. She pondered over Wuthering Heights, as she worked on another Italian sonnet. Emily had died of consumption, and refused to let anyone go for the doctor, she noted at the end. "How unlike my mother also," she thought.

"Even if my mother Ebony knew something was wrong, she would have refused any medical help," thought Ivory. "She had delicate hands and a nightingale mind."

"I think Ebony believed firmly in natural medicine, or my father would not take me to see the naturopath when she died. She was journeying all the time toward the Divine. I even venture she was creating a semblance of the persecuted church in a culture and community where we don't usually see this. Maybe in other cultures, we would see people being thrown in psych wards and persecuted under communism for their beliefs. But not here, not an innocent person," Ivory thought.

It had been her psychiatrist, Dr. Hoffer, who had offered his humble opinion to Ebony. He knew that people contested their treatment, that mental-health certified patients had no rights, and that they certainly could not refuse medication in Canada. Yet he believed Ebony's situation was an example of communism. Dr. Hoffer had given Ebony vitamins, and told her about the use of niacin for mental health patients. She had greatly improved under his care. He was up against the psychiatric community, in pioneering the use of high doses of vitamins; but they had let Ebony go home.

When Ivory knew Dr. Hoffer had another opinion, she understood why he had spent his life helping patients with vitamins. When she believed the basis of orthomolecular medicine, she conceded that her mother could have recovered in her lifetime. If only Dr. Hoffer had not passed away, she thought.

Ivory was almost fifteen and would go to high school soon. She studied her schoolwork in every spare moment. She wanted to study creative writing eventually. She bent over her lined notebook, scrawling in her spiwery handwriting with a pencil:

The variant of each authentic wind beside ocean wall, uniformity of crashing wave, absolving in slight sin a trance of words, the righteous flower to sea: the sunken garden of graduation—a terrace of reparation, each rose. O rebuke me not, absolve my question.

The questions seemed more numerous than the answers. They strung themselves through the galaxy of her thoughts like riddles. And who would answer? This was ponderous; the answers seemed more complicated than the questions. Ivory knew the Divine was a person and heard her prayers, but she wasn't sure the Divine could answer her questions. She was as didactic as she was spiritual, and leaned on science and observation to make up the difference between art and faith. Without her beginning hypothesis, then a step by step proving, how could she come to a winning conclusion?

Protector of my pride from peril's blow, casting of the diamond for each drop dew, noise of the early morning fountain's glow: mother-of-pearl, bedecked in every hue—light lavish, the overripe distance near, karat keeping gem, bright beside each shrub, green jade of each blade, let sorcery hear.

Whoever was listening in, Ivory supposed, knew there was a truth in poetry. It was a truth that was distilled over time, with much cognition. Intellect serving as its protector, with time, truth became wisdom. The depth of wisdom was played out in the very first garden once.

Eve had pondered a rosy fruit, and a serpent had whispered to her that she could be unlike the Divine. It had offered her to eat, when she had been forbidden. Was this the origin of sorcery, in its symbol of evil? Ivory was sure that even now the serpent tempted people with the same seduction.

Was it not the wind that moved the trees? This wordless wind came of an opposite spirit. It offered an invitation, as her friend. There was an invitation she was sure she could ascertain. That invitation was to know the Divine as a person; a person who spoke, and breathed, and walked in her shoes.

O instrument of colors pealing bright the hush of all creation waits for night, for nature's guide to rest each creature's nest; forsythia, here rims each walk at best, the window of a mansion gathers time—cumbersome abode, now heaven be mine—free the linnet from a gilt golden cage.

There seemed a cage of humanity's making that had cast civilization as polite. In all their earthly gestures, humans were often too insecure to think outside the box. Until her mother's death, Ivory had remained firmly within. Now she stood without whilst still in possession of her mother's Oxford Dictionary. With her fiery energy, she strove to become what she was meant to be—a vessel of the Divine.

"Oh mother," she thought, speaking to her mother as though she could hear and were in the room. "When I sit at the black grand piano, my hands hovering over the music, and I play a song that's beating my heart—then I am more than the music perchance, and notes; the rhythms are right here. My home, and the place I belong is just singing.

"When I wait for you in the valley: there you find me, and we walk hand in hand, the winter ground like a crust of jewels. Frozen flowers underfoot, early frost whitening the green flora and fauna, telling the cold time of winter draws near. We will sit by the fire, covered by knit blankets and holding hot tea, warm biscuits, and everything we wished for will seem right here with us, the memories, family and friends who wish us well from a far mile—as love is your lifeline, it just won't die."

Her father was in the next room, and thought, "Chastising me with every drawn-out pirouette of a pen, dipped in ink, black as night, with a few solid stars circling the dark, flaming pure."

"Being a writer is never easy," said Ivory to her father, as she entered the room.

The philosopher looked up. "What do you mean?" he asked casually.

His daughter quoted her mother's verse, "My Lothantique perfume was Ginger, my room spray was of Lavender flower; the white linen room was quietly the most soft-spoken room in the house, and gentlemanly manners prevailed when I then got out my magic pen."

"Aha!" he prevailed around both women with his request for writers and verse, he thought.

"And you, Ivory Snowflake?" he noted. "When the oil of anointing dripped down her forehead each morning, where it had marked the shape of a cross, formally consecrating a small four-year-old, not dissolute, to a deity—and highbrow, she took her books, marched on.

"Opal of valor, appropriate the entire blessed kingdom's moral worth; speak, such a child as would do thy will. And shine words of wisdom in due time, chastening the bitterness, forgive, that then we might be the pure in heart," he finished.

"When she bent over her careful work of writing her lessons in music, her spirit applied itself there to a

Pandora's box of treasures, sent from each winged guardian angel, white, to lift the mind to climb on the heights," quoted his only daughter.

Contemplations of Revelation

O true Friend,
O true revealer of my heart,
O true lattice for my soul's rose,
O joy of my time before heaven,
Braid!

O only prophet
of the logos and the rhema,
(speaker, carrier, listener)
Bind!

O tomb where beauty does not fade,
O epitaph where chiseled in its stone o'er the grave,
Loose!

O Suture of the surgeon's lancet,
O Critique of the artist's paint,
O Map of the compass spiritual quest,
O High places of new worship,
O Beginning from the end, circle us,
Tie!

Section XIII: On The Doorstep

Chapter 41

Ivory went to spend the weekend at her grandparents'
estate on Eagle Mountain. Snowflake Princess missed her
mother more than anything in the world, and thought her
grandparents did also. They had four children, but Ebony
was the eldest. Her Grandmother Velvet's hair was
snowy white, and she made eucalyptus wreaths to hang
on the wall. Ivory could smell the eucalyptus from the
living room, for her grandmother dipped the end of each
sea-green branch in essential oil, then let it dry and added
dried flowers and seed pods.

Her grandmother knew there was symbolism in these
actions. The fragrance would remain long after her
creativity. The people whose lives she touched with her
gifts of homemade ornaments and wreaths knew they
had received a special gift. Her grandmother was a
spiritual person, and even prayed over each of the
recipients of her crafts as she worked.

Ivory sat at the grand piano. Her father had insisted
that she take music lessons growing up, so she knew the
basics of musicianship. She played a two-part invention
by Bach after her scales. Her grandmother listened from
the next room. Really, since her mother's death, her
grandmother was like a mother to her, having her stay

with them every weekend and making batches of cookies. Her grandparents were both reticent and soft-spoken, and her grandfather usually played golf. He was at this moment over at the golf course.

Ivory wandered into the library. She sat down, and wrote in her journal with the fountain pen.

I walked across the driftwood-littered shore—where the sea crashes with ten-year-old impatience, wanting its mother: the moon to dictate its moral conscience.

"I am your father," said the sun. "Drying the land to silt, parching the lips of youth, and lapping at the wake of sea in the early morning, warming the tide pools."

"I am your brother," said the sand. "Sleeping each night from the birds who dig for small insects with their beaks, and the natives who look for clams and mussels."

"I am your sister," said the salt. "And you are the sea: immersed in you, I am forgiving of your lashing wrath and poignant sea-star depths."

The father and mother image demanded more thought, she concluded.

The next weekend when she returned, she wrote again, sitting at the desk in the library:

I am the mother of peoples. I labored many nights and days, to bring you into being here—and now you are my winsome child, captivating as the winter sun over a field of new snow.

Each white snowflake tastes your browned skin, each moment of cold makes your soul sing into the starry night's warmth of our fireside recollections and story of the caribou downwind, a solemn provision.

When we say thank you to salmon and stream, rabbit and pine, berries, and most of all, to deer and fern. Our prayer is to the Creator of each animal and spirit, finding our way across a vast divide—hunger to innocence.

Our father, with a message, travelled from beyond to bring to us the truth of why we labor so long—our tired bodies groaning under the weight of wine and truant hostile outcomes. Why we fail to reap harvest and plenty here, to fill our minds with the positive notes of life.

He said, "Dear friends, remember what you have learned in the school of cultivation and hunting: the gathering of wild roots for centuries, the birthing of children in a dark-cloaked wood, the plenty of squash, beans, and maize in calm rows, the arrowhead and the bright fire of forging.

"The native heritage, an invisible footprint on the forest floor, will lead the way through an impassable wilderness. It will clear the path to an ocean where the surf crashes. It will find you like a mother finds a lost child—weeping salty tears, for she has looked for years."

Ivory's grandparents were Roman Catholic and took her with them to mass on Sundays. She usually wore a skirt and blouse, combed her hair neatly and braided it down her back. Her grandfather placed the sign of the cross in olive oil on her forehead and the anointing was supposed to protect her in this life. They sat in the pew at St. Ann's and listened to the priest. She fingered the tiny silver St. Christopher's medal around her throat.

The priest continued: "You are the altar on which I am sacrificed on rough stones... praying like a bird in a cage... steeling my forehead as a farmer does when his plough must go forward... seeing the sun drop in the sky.

"And the clouds ever-move, sculpted by the master—drifting from one thought to the next, composed. The rain falls, on dormant worlds and high-strung gardens: a cellist sits on the wall and plays toward evening.

"You are the womb of life and when I am born I am firmly in your grasp. Holding me to the breast is the mother of life, and the breath in me must go forward... 'till death lays me in a field."

The service was over. They all filed out one by one, shaking the Father's hand. They headed home in her grandparents' stately car. Ivory thought of her mother's patchwork quilt as she watched the countryside go by.

Later, Ivory followed the cobblestone path around to the garden. The softened caress of evening moved the last light to portraiture beyond human doubt, despondency, and despair. A moment's wind dappled the surface of the fountain's clay colored waters. Ivory looked and watched her reflection for a moment.

There were four stone walls around the garden. As she observed the walls, she felt as if her own heart had walls of stone also. She must be made of stone within, she surmised, and wondered if the rock would ever melt. If it did, she would love and be loved in return, she felt sure. Her emotions rose, a blue moon over the garden. She was a shadowy garden of poetry, with each flower yet to be discovered. Suet hung in a small black cage for the nightingales.

The sighing wind of self-pity blew, which often made a slave of women who were dutiful. The drenching rain of depression trickled, that could root one to the ground if deemed only for the menial labors of cooking and cleaning. Ivory was glad she was a writer unlike her mother, but knew her grandparents might not agree with her choice. They believed a woman should marry well, or have a solid profession. Her mother had married the philosopher, and they were usually silent at this.

She thought, "I lifted my hair and posed for the medieval lens: melodic, sonorous, clothed in burgundy dress with rose wreath of twenty-four white roses and four, red as my lips."

Nature seemed an open book. Constellations, trees, flowers of every variety, and animals, down to the insects inhabiting the ground, were fair game for humanity lessons. She had poured over the garden, unlike her mother's photograph exhibits. Her mother had always said that human nature and nature mirrored each other.

Now, at dusk, Ivory could sense there was something practical yet surreal about the garden, drawing her like a Pandora 's box. Something about the garden was speaking in the night, and she felt its docile politeness and inhuman wilds both at once. The hours often spoke themselves through her pen. Yet they had not before spoken to her in evensong such fervency through her evening rambles. An owl flew overhead.

She continued her thought, "I paused—and the dreams of summer melted in the field. My sisters gathered 'round with prayers—to make me fortified, steadfast as the sacred cross, where pathos had not gone before."

Ivory walked until she found one small sacred glen, where light from the sky was shaded by one still mossy tree. Here she stood, blinking through the shadow world, kin to all enchanted fairy meadows. She took notice to note the moment's verse, still unbeknownst until this late hour. The stone sundial would tell the time, and spy on the imperative, their goodly cry.

When she returned to her bedroom, she braided her hair by the window. As she did, she watched the owls rise into the trees, pure snowy white, their eyes blinking soberly at light. Each planet, star, and moon festooned demure to hang in navy-black seas of night. Ships dipped in the waves of mystic cursive where she scribbled down each last thought.

Oh here, by this small book where ink meets the line of page, and sorrow meets joy, and humor, mirth—come with me in this final hour, the world mine, and find the journey home, the land uncursed where spirit meets the soul of man. Where soul reads last, his lantern lit over the tome, the ghost no fancy of the literate mind, here glass.

"There are two sides to everyone, just like the two sides of a chessboard," she thought, "white and black. Her only fault was she believed there was good in everyone." With that, she closed her journal and hopped into the feather bed.

 **Chapter 42**

Snowflake Princess sat in her desk in English class, laboring over an essay. Her teacher had asked them to write their final paper on their philosophy of life. She had thought about it for a while, and then wrote:

I am walking through life, fortified, won by the circle of kindness of the great people, those I have met along the way who have been battered by adversity, who know the call of hard perseverance. Battered by time, they have improvised love.

The clear quality of being hard-pressed is the subtle nature of becoming a diamond, hard enough to cut through what the world would deem impenetrable. Those who would follow in this way, come now, come forward, find the way through rough sorrow.

My mantra is this: I will forgive my own injustice, my birth, my hatred, my faults, and my life will have purpose and meaning in the depth of love.

Forget not what I have said and you will live; throw out my words, and the worst may befall you. The flag of a nation is its pride, do not let it drag in the dust, do not let it fall. Sing the anthem with lustrous vigor.

I will say my mantra over society, leaving a thin mist of grace over the rice fields. Hanging low, the words permeate, carefully written—all scoffers shake their heads, stop, slow and yield; the pen on folded sheets of translucent paper, the writing scratched and fine, bearing incense, flowing onward to the beat of time's drum and tapered light.

Sesame oil was poured out—ginger reducing in coconut milk simmered over a bright flame, with vegetables in rainbow hues, seducing palate of the level-headed, those with no blame. The irony that men would work until work was done. That dark women would wash their hair in the river—the beggar, brandishing his tin to beg for one.

And I would not consort to make a lengthy law that all must follow, to present their case as truth. Right here, under the golden sun, reapers—raw as the dust, looking for one eternal home, truce to every religion, while steady Buddhists pray—meditation of a moment, standing for zeal: mentoring an homage to rebirth, day by day.

Ivory walked down St. Charles Avenue with the philosopher. They had taken a ferry over to the island on

her spring break. She was delighted with this turn of
events, and the chance to camp by the ocean in tents.

"In every studied word let there be nourishment to the
veins of auburn earth, great victory, and discourse to
unearth, a veritable map to cross each sea," he said.

At Rockland Avenue, there was the old mansion. Its
empty rooms were silent, but its eyes still winked of light
by day and night. Her mother had been a patient here in
Victoria once, writing a poem by candlelight. She had
been studious throughout her life, and silent at life's
rejection, but never her pen. Her pen would always speak
up for her silenced voice. Her pen resounded like the
outward circles after a stone on Hayward lake. Ivory had
the torn piece of paper, yellowed over the years.

The silver bird that eats the apples, red,
perches on the boughs, sings loud, bright and gay,
I woke and listened to his call from bed—
revived my spirit where my body lay.
Never have I heard such joyous song laud:
the simple worship of a creature, bare
to his redemption heaven would applaud,
and reap the bettering of life with care.
In each new day, the rich scent of the pines,
the forest brook which bubbles, frothy, cold—
attempt to give my soul all that is mine,
and retell in myth all I have been told.
I stretch my hands out from my infirm room
where I knew only bleak estate of doom.

An apple tree flowered out by the ocean and Ivory sat under it for a while, trying to recover what was lost. She and the philosopher made their camp here by the sea. They cooked at the Coleman stove on the picnic table. She had wanted to read the story again. "Is there still a copy around of *Red Velvet Cake*?" she asked.

A small blonde head was out in the fields. A golden horse came down the hill as she approached the pasture. The young girl stretched out her hand. Strong as a sequoia, she was like Queen Anne's lace among the silver grasses that grow along the coast of Vancouver Island.

The mansion stood empty. The second house had been sold for a tea room, and the garden, now abandoned, afforded no clue. They lifted the knocker and gave the door a tap tap but no one responded. In front, the fountain still trickled beside the statue of St. Francis.

Someone with a big heart had spoken into the night about taming a wild horse once, and a community of care workers had listened. It had changed the way anorexics were cared for. The wild horse was hunger. It could destroy a family, and shatter a world. Yet it was the same hunger that fed the poor of refugee camps, and drilled wells in the desert. When the wild horse was tamed, food would become an ally instead of an enemy. Children would come neatly dressed to the table for meals.

It seemed impossible that the children of tomorrow would know how to heal the wound of society without the two mansions of City of Roses. They represented the two mansions of the soul: heaven's mansion of unconditional love, and earth's mansion of unrequited love. Ivory did not wish for the next generation to be subject to the third mansion, where the door closed behind you, forgotten love. Usually she had only to apply her will to find a solution. The old house, when empty, spoke of pain and abandonment. Why was it shut down, she wondered, when it had helped so many? The questions between Ivory and the philosopher lingered long after everyone had gone home.

"I am dedicated to paradise and its childlike door that I opened once, looking for more than my story book offered —I walked through and was clothed, divine in nature's hues, crimson, golden," she thought.

Ivory had a pen and paper. She hoped to enter the creative writing program at university in a year. Her father knew she was hunting to find out more about her mother's background. Only the old German film of her mother had afforded a clue. The ocean was still breathing its silent remorse. She left a solitary poem on the doorstep, "How To Catch A Wild Horse."

Contemplations of Revelation

O true Presence,
O true healer,
O true voice,
O spirit of contemplation,
Rejoice!

O only builder
of the three mansions of the soul,
(heaven, earth, hell)
Restore!

O highest beauty of all created things,
O paradise of the seven heavens,
Repair!

O Subject of the child's dream,
O Object of the prophet's word,
O Deeps of onward wisdom,
O Healer of the Mother wound,
O Tryst with triune light,
Reunite!

About the Author

Emily Isaacson was born December 11, 1975 in Windsor, Ontario and grew up in Victoria, B.C., Canada. She is both Scottish (on the maternal side) and German, (on the paternal side), and has a Scottish plaid. Emily Isaacson studied nutrition at Bastyr University of natural medicine where she received her Bachelor of Science.

Emily Isaacson began writing poetry at age ten, where she lived not far from the sea on Vancouver Island. She was first published at age thirteen for her poem, "The Wild Madonna". She has now published over 1,800 poems in eight books of poetry, establishing her as a beloved Canadian author.

Isaacson is founder and director of The Emily Isaacson Institute in the Fraser Valley. She spent five years there writing her life work, The Fleur-de-lis, a three volume work of over 800 poems. She now serves as an arts advocate.

Praise for The Fleur-de-lis:

Emily Isaacson, in The Fleur-de-lis, embraces Canada's history and views it through the fresh lens of poetry. Her voice is passionate, multi-colored, and lyrical. Her skilled and accessible verses show that the reach of her understanding is deeper than fact-finding; they turn this telling into a document to be celebrated.

Luci Shaw, poet
Author of Harvesting Fog